"THE WATER SUCKED HER UNDER AGAIN.

Her lungs felt as though they were bursting. She struggled in terror. Someone was turning her on her back, starting to swim with her. . . .

"When she regained consciousness, he was kissing her, she decided. . . . She couldn't breathe this way, or return his kiss.

" 'I'm okay.' Her eyes opened slowly.

"He had gray eyes and his unruly black hair was damp from the water.

This was Michelle Lambert's first good look at Dr. Rick Prentice. She owed him her life.

Would he want her love?

Other SIGNET Nurse-Doctor Titles

Nurse Lambert's Conflict

by
Diana Douglas

A Signet Book

Published by The New American Library
in association with Horowitz Publications

SIGNET TRADEMARK REG. U.S. PAT. OFF. AND FOREIGN COUNTRIES
REGISTERED TRADEMARK—MARCA REGISTRADA
HECHO EN CHICAGO, U.S.A.

SIGNET BOOKS are published by
The New American Library, Inc.,
1301 Avenue of the Americas, New York, New York 10019

FIRST PRINTING, DECEMBER, 1969

PRINTED IN THE UNITED STATES OF AMERICA

chapter one

Opiates had washed out both pain and reality so that the man in the bed lay quiet, breathing heavily and deeply. Beside him, Michelle Lambert finished her routine checking and began her notation on the patient's chart. She could hear the other duty nurse, Betty Falkiner, on the other side of the screen, wheeling her dressing cart along the line of beds with Dr. Moreton, one of Hillside's interns, and joking with the patients as she worked.

At first Nurse Lambert barely noticed the slow footsteps and low voices. Two other men had come into the ward and stopped near her patient's bed. She recognized Dr. Creighton's voice, but the other was unknown to her.

"If I'd suspected, I would have returned home long ago, George," a deep unfamiliar voice said quietly.

"None of us suspected it, Rick. But *he* knew. He was carrying tablets. But he didn't tell your sister or me. We found cardiographs among his papers afterwards. And of course the attack came when he was in a patient's house. There just wasn't anything we could do. I was out on a case, and Dr. Meredith was in the middle of a splenectomy. Myers went out on the ambulance and did all he could to revive him. But it was hopeless, just one of those things. If it had happened here, your father might have had a chance. It was just fate, I'm afraid."

Nurse Lambert had finished now, but tact held her behind the screen, frowning slightly as she listened to their voices. They were discussing Hillside's late owner and medical superintendent, Dr. Henry Prentice, known to everyone as Dr. Henry.

"If only I'd come back sooner, and taken some of the pressure off Dad . . ."

"Rick, we see such things happen all the time," Creighton said. "*If* the letter he sent you hadn't gone astray. *If* you hadn't been already in Australia when they tried to contact you in Vietnam. *If* the patient's wife had known he carried the tablets when he had the attack. *If* Myers had managed to get to him in time with the oxygen. Hell, Rick, let's leave it. Myers will tell you more when you meet him."

After a troubled silence the deep voice said, "You're right, George. And he went out the way he always said he wanted to. Working . . ."

"Helping someone who needed him," George Creighton said gruffly. "Or trying to. But you'll want to hear about the clinic. He was doing some wonderful work on arterial grafts just before it happened. Some of the things he did created a lot of interest—even outside San Francisco—and he kept meticulous records, obviously with your return in mind. He even managed to add another wing." They walked on slowly. "You'll meet a lot of new people here—Carter and Richardson, house surgeons, and of course the nurses come and go. But all the old stalwarts are still with us. Miss Pringle, the Director of the Nursing Service, and the house mother, Mrs. Patterson."

"And Lisa Grahame?"

"Your dad's scrub nurse? No. Lisa left three months ago. Married a resident over at the Medical Center. She was helping out at your father's office downtown. We have a Miss Lambert in her place. Younger than Lisa. But good. You remember how particular your father was about his instrument nurse? Well, he tried several

6

after Lisa left, drove them to tears, literally, before this one came along. She only worked with him for a few weeks, but he told me confidentially that she is as good as Lisa was at her age. Coming from him, that was quite a compliment."

"If she won him over, she must be good."

"She is good. And here's a surprise for you—she's also attractive. Remember what he used to say about nurses? That it was what they could do that counted, not how they looked. He used to say that a pretty girl distracted everyone from patients to medical staff, including herself. But he seems to have made an exception in Michelle's case. I believe she made him feel young again. When you meet her you'll know what I mean. And it isn't all sex."

The nurse moved uneasily. Her face flushed slightly, and she wished they'd move away.

"Michelle?" the deep voice said. "She isn't French?"

"No. Born in Boston. Studied nursing in the East. She was Henderson's scrub nurse at Bellevue. I understand Henderson recommended her personally when she applied for the job here. Said he was sorry to lose her."

"What's she like? I mean, to look at?"

Creighton chuckled. "This one is certainly interesting, but don't quote me to Mary. She's small and neat. A sort of pocket Venus. How would you describe her? She has the face of a Spanish virgin, olive-skinned, serious, with big velvet-brown eyes. A Mona Lisa smile. There's sadness in her. Henderson mentioned some personal reason for her wanting to leave Bellevue, so there's probably a broken romance in the background."

"I didn't know you could be so lyrical, George."

"About this girl I can. But I want to show you the new wing of the clinic. You know, Rick, our problem here is that we are a small hospital struggling to carry the heavy expense and responsibility of a free clinic. It's just too heavy a burden for us."

"It was what my father wanted, George."

They were moving away now. The nurse stirred and glanced from her patient to the space between the

7

screen and the wall. In a moment now she could escape without embarrassment.

Dr. Creighton's voice, fading, said, "Sure, and we all know how much the clinic meant to Dr. Henry, Rick. But it's a matter of finance. The hospital can't afford to carry it much longer. What with rising costs and the influx of patients needing surgery, it's anyone's guess how long the clinic can survive."

"It must survive, George. It's needed here . . ."

Nurse Lambert let her breath out slowly. She began to smile. Face of a Spanish virgin, she thought. Is that the way I look to Dr. Creighton? And a Mona Lisa smile?

She shook her head and adjusted the screen before she automatically glanced along the ward. The electronic panel at the end of the ward was flashing Dr. Creighton's number, indicating that he was wanted urgently in Ward Three, bed seventeen.

The dressing cart had reached the end of the ward, and the intern was talking to the patient in the end bed.

"Dr. Creighton wants to cut and ligate your varicose veins, Mr. Peel. As he told you, your condition is too advanced for injections now. But there's nothing to worry about. Eighty percent of cases like yours get excellent results from surgery, and the other twenty percent are improved. It's not a dangerous operation. The danger would be if you didn't have it done."

"Suppose I didn't?" The patient was staring up at him uncertainly.

"Well, you could get a deep ulceration that might refuse to heal. Infections might develop, perhaps even with phlebitis—that's inflammation of the veins. You wouldn't want that?"

"If Dr. Henry was here . . ."

"He isn't, so it has to be Dr. Creighton," the intern smiled. "Dr. Creighton is an excellent surgeon. And you know that he has assisted Dr. Prentice for so long that operations like yours aren't going to trouble him. Now just lie back and relax. Dr. Creighton will see you again tonight before he leaves. Remember, the operation isn't

8

painful, except where the cuts are made, and that isn't going to hurt for long at all. You may not even have to stay in bed afterward, and you can expect to go home in a couple of days."

"All the same, I'd feel better about it if old Dr. Henry was around . . ."

"They all say the same thing in these damn clinic wards," the intern muttered disgustedly as he walked away. "You'd think Peel was paying thousands of dollars to have his varicose veins reduced. What the hell do people like that have to bitch about?"

"They don't have to have a reason Dr. Moreton," Betty Falkiner said, walking beside him. "And you'd better not let Dr. Creighton hear you. Or Dr. Meredith. Say, do you know who that was who came into the ward with Dr. Creighton just now, Barry?"

"The tall guy? No. Is he a doctor?" He stopped at the office and looked back. "Maybe Miss Ward will know. She's been here long enough to know everyone." He broke off, studying the nurse approaching them, an admiring glint in his blue eyes. "Hello, Miss Lambert. I thought it was Miss Ward back there with Nine. What are you doing out of O.R.?"

"Miss Ward asked me to stand in for her," Michelle Lambert explained. "She isn't feeling well."

"Did you notice who it was with Creighton back there?"

"I couldn't see him. But Dr. Creighton called him Rick, and he referred to Dr. Prentice as Dad, so . . ." She left it at that.

"Rick Prentice?" Dr. Moreton's blue eyes studied her. "Are you sure, Miss Lambert?"

"They have been expecting him home, Doctor."

"That's right. It must be Prentice. Now maybe we'll get some action around here."

Michelle Lambert smiled. "Why? I thought we already had all the action we could handle at Hillside with so many patients coming to Casualty."

"That's just it," Moreton said soberly. "If we had half the number of Casualty patients we're getting now we'd have more than our share. Too many of them get shuttled here that should be going to the big public hospitals. We're a private show at Hillside, sort of family hospital for a group of doctors in private practice, with a specialty clinic for arterial surgery that's second to none, or wasn't while Dr. Henry was alive! But now we're getting bogged down with road casualties, and nobody seems to know what to do about it." He sighed and ran his hand over his thick blond hair.

"*And* we're understaffed," Betty Falkiner said. "And we don't have enough accommodation, or amenities, or equipment. And we don't have the money to get them."

Moreton glanced at her indignant face and grinned. "And *that* just about sums it up, Miss Lambert. Although maybe you haven't noticed these things from the O.R.?"

She frowned. The duties of the operating room staff did keep them apart from the other services at Hillside. Surgery had been Dr. Henry Prentice's lifework. Most of the really good equipment at Hillside was in the surgical services.

She shrugged. "That isn't unusual, Doctor."

"No, maybe it isn't. Well, Rick Prentice is an outstanding surgeon. I've read some of his papers on arterial grafts. So he'll probably follow Dr. Henry's line. But he has something Dr. Henry didn't have. He's been in charge of a modern military hospital in Vietnam, and one a lot bigger than this. So he's a trained organizer. I hope he remembers that, and doesn't get as involved with the clinic as his father was. There are other things in medicine beside what the cut-and-sew boys do, Miss Lambert. Little things like obstetrics and gynecology, psychiatry, pediatrics, and medicine, real medicine, which means the diagnosis and treatment of the sick by other means than surgery."

"Perhaps he'll remember that, Dr. Moreton," she said quietly.

He signed Betty Falkiner's ward sheet, and grinned at them both. "Forgive the sermon, Miss Lambert."

She smiled. "I can see your point, Dr. Moreton. And I hope things will improve for you now."

"I think I should advise you, Miss Lambert, that I am merely a humble intern, Barry Moreton M.D. (practicing provisionally)."

"I'd no idea," Michelle replied. "I thought you were an attending at least."

"Isn't she sweet?" he asked Betty Falkiner. "I don't suppose we could persuade her to abandon the O.R. for the medical service wards?"

"Not if she has any sense," Betty Falkiner smiled. "And besides, she's too pretty. There's enough competition around here already."

"Which reminds me, Harker wants me in the children's ward after this and he's likely to can our Saturday night date if I keep him waiting."

"I'll can *you* if you let him!" Betty Falkiner threatened fiercely.

Michelle laughed as he hurried out. "He's nice."

"I think so," Betty said, studying his thickset, sturdy figure hurrying toward the elevators. The warm expression in her large gray eyes accentuated her soft, smooth cheeks. Her complexion was creamy, but slightly dark, and her round, small face was very attractive.

"Are you going steady?" Michelle asked.

"Yes, I suppose we are. At least we see as much of each other as we can, and neither of us is interested in anyone else. But it isn't easy to get together. You have to have the same time off duty, and Barry's an intern. Hillside isn't different from any other hospital where interns are concerned. The residents are tough on them. I'm never sure whether Barry will get away, or if Dr. Harker, his senior resident, will make him take a different shift."

"Well, what's next on the roster?" Michelle asked brightly.

"Closets, and some sterilizing. I'll start in while you make us both a cup of coffee, if you like."

"Do you want coffee now?"

"Gotta be quick around here," Betty replied, with a

11

definite nod of her head. "Take your coffee while you may. Who knows when the worthy Pringle will walk in? She has a thing about these wards. We're entitled to our coffee break, *but* . . ."

Michelle nodded her understanding. "We see quite a lot of the Director too. Usually after it's over and we're cleaning up."

"Ugh!" Betty Falkiner shuddered. "My stint up in O.R. almost decided me that I wasn't meant to be a nurse. Honestly, doesn't it get you sometimes, Michelle?"

"Sometimes. Mostly though I think about my feet. The rest is more or less automatic, unless you get an emergency. Everything is practically decided before you start. Well, I'll make that coffee. Won't be long."

When Michelle opened the door of her room in the Nurses' Home, Carla Simon, her roommate was already in bed, reading.

"Hi! You look bushed," Carla said as she put her book aside.

"Hi! I feel it." Michelle kicked off her shoes and sat down. She stretched her legs and wiggled her toes, studying them sympathetically.

"Anything interesting around the wards?" Carla asked.

"No. Just patients, closets, and sterilizing. Why?"

"You missed something by not being at dinner to-night. Dr. Prentice is back from Vietnam to take over his father's place. And is he marvelous!"

Michelle lifted one foot and began to massage her toes through her stocking. "He is?" Right then a nice hot shower and bed were her major interests.

"Marvelous isn't the word. Beautiful is more like it!" Carla looked at her enthusiastically. "No guy has a right to be *that* good-looking *and* unmarried."

"For heaven's sake, Carla!" Don't sound so desperate."

The vivacious girl ignored her, and went on enthusiastically. "Dr. Creighton introduced him to every-

12

one. Of course, he knew a lot of people. He interned here, you know."

"No, I didn't know that."

"Then he did his residency in the army, and stayed in for a second two year stint. He's tall and has dark hair, also an unbelievable suntan, and the grayest eyes ever. He's a dream!"

"Right now the only dream I want is with my eyes closed."

"Say, what's the matter with you? You don't even sound mildly excited, and every girl in the nursing service is raving about him. At least all those who saw him tonight."

"Maybe that's why," Michelle said wearily. "I didn't see him tonight, and all I can think about is putting my feet up and my head down. I'll feel better after I've soaked out some of the tiredness."

"Sorry," Carla said. "Forgot you've been standing in. You go off to the showers. I'll go and get us some coffee from the canteen."

Michelle undressed quickly, slipped into a robe, threw a towel over her shoulder and limped to the bathroom. She ran the shower hot and hard upon her firm young body, closing her eyes in bliss as the steam writhed up above her to make damp patches on the ceiling. The warmth of the water eased away her fatigue.

When she returned to their room, Carla was waiting with the coffee, still intent upon discussing Dr. Rick Prentice. She was still talking about him when Michelle's eyes closed slowly and she drifted into sleep.

The last words that registered in her mind became a part of her dreaming.

"You're going to be closer to him than anyone else, Michelle. But if you do become interested, don't think you're not going to have competition. Darling, you'll have plenty."

She wakened with a start and sat up abruptly. Sunshine streamed through the windows. She turned her head anxiously and was relieved to find Carla Simon's blue eyes studying her quizzically over a paperback from the other bed.

"Thought you were going to sleep forever," she said, shaking her head. "How do you manage it? I believe you could sleep hung on a clothes line!"

"Have I overslept? Heavens, what time is it?" Michelle reached for the small, leather-covered traveling clock beside her bed, and gasped in dismay. "Ten o'clock? Carla!" she said accusingly, "I should have been in the O.R. preparing at eight-thirty!"

Carla giggled. "Wake up, darling! That was yesterday. Remember? Today is Saturday, and we're on stand-by this morning, but from noon until Monday morning we're both as free as the breeze."

"Oh, God!" Michelle muttered. "For a minute there I even forgot what year it was."

"Do you think I'd have let you sleep late, and that both our house mother and Director of Nursing Service had neglected to notice that the O.R. was without its scrub nurse and circulating nurse? Really, sweet! Pringle would have had battering rams beating down our door hours ago. How a girl as bright as you can sleep so deeply and wake up in such a state of utter confusion, I'll never know!"

"Sometimes you burn me up, Carla," Michelle muttered resentfully. "Have you been reading that book all night?"

"No. But it's good. A Gothic. The innocent heroine arrives at a big old house by the sea and is beset by all kinds of perils in the dark and gloomy passages where evil creatures lurk in wait for her and cobwebs trail from the ceilings. This one is *weird*!"

"The last book I read was Baker's Endocrinology. Recommended reading for post-graduate classes."

"You'd find this one more interesting."

"I'll bet." Michelle put out a long slim leg to test the temperature. Warm. Warm enough for swimming. "Are you going up to your folks' beach house at Bolinas this weekend, Carla?" she asked wistfully.

Michelle felt that Carla was a lucky girl, although

much too spoiled. Her people were wealthy, and she had a car, and the beach house. She was not really pretty, but she had a neat figure and lively blue eyes that went with her blond hair. Men liked Carla, and so did most of the girls who worked with her.

Carla looked at Michelle closely, aware of the loneliness behind her question. She remembered that Michelle had not made many friends yet at Hillside; she was too quiet and too shy.

Of course, Carla remembered, she had half promised Bryan Meredith a date that night . . . "Why yes," she said. "It should be a perfect weekend for the beach. Would you like to come with me?"

Michelle looked at her, startled. "It's awfully nice of you to ask me, Carla, but I couldn't."

"You have a date?"

"No. But I couldn't intrude like that. Your parents . . ."

"Won't be there," Carla said, putting down her book. "There will only be the two of us. If you can't come I'll spend the weekend here at the hospital. It's no fun going alone. But I really *would* like to show you Bolinas and Surfside, as Dad calls the cottage. It's terrific. The beach is very private and quite safe. There are about a dozen cottages, but one or two are never used. Actually, it's a few miles from Bolinas, near Twin Heads. The beach is called Silver Sands."

"It sounds fabulous," Michelle said.

"Then you'll come? Honestly, Michelle, you'll love it."

"When would you leave?" she asked doubtfully.

"We could go at noon. I was down there last week, and there's plenty of food. No need to buy a thing. All we have to do is get up and go. We can stay there Sunday night and drive back to the hospital early Monday morning. How about it, Michelle?"

The last of her resistance faded and Michelle slid out of bed to embrace her friend happily.

"Carla, you're a darling! It sounds wonderful!"

15

"Then let's shower and get ready for a flying start when the clock strikes twelve."

Carla stretched like a cat waking from a sleep in the sun, yawned and put her book where she would be sure not to forget it. Michelle had opened the drapes and was looking down toward the hospital entrance across the green lawns, now in early summer and bright with flowers. Carla studied her in silhouette against the window with just a twinge of envy, as well as a warm feeling of admiration. With the light gleaming on her raven hair, and her figure glimpsed through the thin nightdress, she was strikingly beautiful. No nurse had a right to look like that. She should be modeling or on her way to stardom in the movies.

"You won't see him down there," Carla said mischievously, reaching for her robe and slippers. "They're having a board meeting today to discuss ways and means of keeping this show on the road."

"See who?" Michelle asked.

"Rick Prentice, of course. The guy you were so uninterested in last night. But that's his car near the entrance. The same Chrysler Dr. Henry Prentice drove. They say he's taking over Dr. Henry's uptown apartment, as well as his practice. All of which makes him a very eligible bachelor, you must agree!"

Michelle nodded faintly and turned away from the window, thinking again of the weekend ahead . . .

It was as though he hadn't been away at all, Rick Prentice decided as he sat at the head of the long boardroom table. Except that his father was not here, and he himself sat in his father's place. The faces around the table were the same, the things they discussed so anxiously were also the same. For as long as he could remember, Hillside Hospital had been struggling financially. It had gone a little further in debt of late, that was the only difference. But his father had felt strongly that service to the sick was much more important than financial solvency.

Listening to one board member after the other, Rick

16

could see quite clearly why his father, who had worked so hard for so long, had left only a few thousand dollars, the practice, and the car. The old doctor had stinted himself for years in order to build the Hillside Clinic.

Creighton knew, they all knew. Creighton was saying, "Henry spent every cent he could raise to build the new clinic wing, and most of us went in deeper than we could afford to help him do it. So the new wing was built, and now it puts Hillside deeper in the red every day."

Rick said slowly, "There's another way of looking at that, George. Even if it did impoverish my father, it enriched the profession of medicine. In Vietnam many of the techniques we used in arterial reconstructive surgery originated right here at Hillside. They were Dad's techniques, evolved meticulously over the years. And some of you helped him do that. You, George, for one. Bryan Meredith, Carter, Richardson, and others who stayed a while and moved on years ago. God knows how many lives those techniques have saved in Vietnam—and are saving now."

George Creighton nodded. "Yes, that's true. And don't think badly of anyone here, Rick. Each of us privately has given more than he can afford to keep the clinic running, without any hope of recovering it. The thing is, Rick, how much longer can we do this?"

"I can't answer that," Rick said slowly. "But I'll promise you one thing—if it's possible to put Hillside in the position to run the clinic without private support from board members, I mean to do it. I've one suggestion I want you to think about between now and our next meeting. But first, I intend to take up part of the debt myself. I have Dad's practice, and that's enough for me. I'm prepared to start from there with a small working capital of, say, five thousand. I'll convert some stock into cash, Dad's as well as my own, but the whole of it is going to help get Hillside in the black. It should be around thirty thousand dollars."

"You're doing what the rest of us have been doing, Rick, plowing your personal profits into the clinic. It

17

isn't good business. Not from your viewpoint. And it will be the last you'll see of your thirty grand."

Bryan Meredith had said that. He had looked up from doodling on a pad while he listened. The youngest board member other than Rick, he was attending at Hillside Surgical Service, its acting chief now since the senior Dr. Prentice died.

"I'm giving it to Hillside as a gift, Bryan," Rick said. "I don't expect or want it back. Some of it is Dad's money, and I know that's what he would want done with it. Now here's the suggestion. I met Arthur Dickinson in town this morning. Arthur, as you all know, is our leading obstetrician. He has his own hospital in town, but it's small, and it's only leased, so Arthur can't extend the building. He needs more beds and more staff. As it is, he sends his cesareans to us. And he has one of the biggest practices in town. Well look here, we have three wards in the new clinic wing, and they're all large. I suggest we take one ward, sound-proof one end for a labor ward, and invite Arthur to move in. Obstetrical equipment in comparison to surgical equipment costs little. And obstetrical costs are government guaranteed. I mentioned the idea to him, and he agreed in principle. And with an obstetric ward in the new wing, the city authorities won't be able to send so many road casualties to us. Beds have to be held for mothers."

"I don't see how we can refuse, Rick. After all, we have one practically empty ward most of the time. I'm all for it," George Creighton said enthusiastically. "This might bring us close to breaking even by the end of the year."

"Anybody object?"

"Object?" Meredith asked, grinning. "Rick, do you have any other ideas like that one?"

"Give Arthur that ward and he'll have twice as many beds, as well as better equipment," Carter said. "He'd need assistance. With his reputation, the ward will be overflowing."

"We'll give him assistance," Rick said.

"Arthur has an ambulance, but we might need another."

"Then we'll get one. With the debt reduced, that shouldn't be difficult," Meredith said. "Look, why don't we go on with this right away? Before some other hospital grabs Arthur away from us. I move that the secretary draft a letter to Dr. Arthur Dickinson inviting him to discuss the matter with us at the first convenient date."

Rick walked out of the boardroom with Bryan Meredith and George Creighton after the resolution had been carried unanimously.

"Nobody wants to make big profits from Hillside," George Creighton was saying as they came down the steps. "But I've always thought that Dr. Henry was making a mistake in expanding the clinic too fast. It would have been better to build the clinic slowly, from hospital profits preferably. That way, you keep the hospital as a whole out of debt."

Meredith agreed. "Find another bright idea like that one, Rick, and this could happen."

"I mean to try."

The two men with him stopped near a black Chrysler. George Creighton glanced at his watch. "I'll have to leave you. Mary is expecting me home for lunch. Office patients afterwards, and I've promised to take her to a show tonight. Are you coming to dinner Sunday, Rick? You're welcome, you know. Must be pretty grim for you in the apartment just now."

Rick smiled, but shook his head. "Tell Mary no thanks. Not this weekend. I have some settling in to do before starting work Monday."

"I thought you started work today," Creighton grinned. "And it seemed to me you made a pretty good start, eh Bryan?"

"He's right, Rick," Meredith said, as Creighton walked away, "about not staying in the apartment this weekend. Remember the beach house your father built out at Bolinas? You and I used to go down there to fish and swim when we were doing our residency here. He never sold it, you know. Why don't we go down there and take a look this weekend? See if the place is still standing."

"Silver Sands Beach," Rick said slowly. "I haven't thought about it for years." He was remembering how close he and Bryan Meredith had been in those days. The war had certainly changed things.

"Well?"

Rick grinned. "I'd like that, Bryan." It suddenly occurred to him that he didn't even know whether his friend had married or not. He added, "What about you? Can you get away?"

Bryan Meredith laughed. "You aren't the only one who's been too busy to find a wife, man. There's a girl in your surgical team that I take out now and then. A blonde named Carla, but there's no problem. We didn't have anything definite planned for this weekend."

"George introduced me to Carla last night," Rick acknowledged.

Bryan glanced up at the Nurses' Home and grinned. "Hey!" he exclaimed. "She's looking down at us from the window right now!" He raised his hand in a wave. "That's Michelle Lambert with her. She's your scrub nurse."

Rick shaded his eyes as he looked up at the window, but the dark-haired girl withdrew quickly when she saw him staring at her.

"I'll pick you up at four o'clock then," Bryan said. "I bet we'll have a great weekend."

chapter two

"When I was an intern I thought about getting married. But what intern can really afford it?" Meredith said, sipping his cold beer. "As a resident I thought of it too and couldn't afford it then either. I was starting to plan the establishment of a practice about then, and that takes money."

They had broken their journey for a drink in a bar overlooking a long stretch of beach.

"I had the same problems you did as an intern," Rick smiled. "And my residency was busy, to say the least. I was with a forward unit for a while, so there didn't seem much sense in planning a future. Afterward, when I was given a hospital to look after, I was too busy. There was still enough element of risk to make the future uncertain. You could never be sure the Vietcong would not sneak in close, set up their mortars and . . . *wham*! Too many unpleasant things were possible to make thoughts of marriage practicable then."

"And now?"

"From what I heard at the board meeting Bryan, I seem to have inherited another set of problems. Less dangerous maybe, but equally demanding. Later maybe."

"I've felt the same way," Bryan Meredith frowned. "About Hillside, I mean. I'm beginning to think it's a mistake, Rick. If we don't watch out we'll wake up one morning and find it's later than we think."

Rick laughed. "Say, what brought this on? Were you thinking about Miss What's-her-name? The blond girl?"

"Carla Simon?" Meredith frowned. "No, of course not," he said, too vehemently. "I hope the refrigerator is still working. I'm going to get us some beer. Fishing can be thirsty work."

"If the fishing gear is still there."

"If it isn't, we'll buy more," Meredith said. "We'll be doing this again, Rick."

The car climbed over a steep ridge and swooped down the other side with Silver Sands ahead in the distance. The place had grown in his absence. Where there had been a half dozen houses there were now twenty. There was a store, and a gas station. He found it difficult to recognize the cottage among the trees.

"Do you have a key?" Bryan asked.

"There's a Mexican family that has one; but don't expect too much. I couldn't find any record of cleaning fees among Dad's accounts."

"We'll make out okay," Bryan said cheerfully.

"We can sleep on the cruiser, if he hasn't sold it, or the Ortez family might put us up." He had forgotten the small cabin cruiser. It had been his father's pride, all new paint and gleaming brass. It seemed strange that he had forgotten it. He decided that it had probably gone long ago to help pay the costs of the clinic.

"It probably went," Bryan said. "Like everything else he had, the clinic swallowed it. He might have lived longer, Rick, if he had come down here more often. Do you remember how fond he was of this place and the cruiser?"

"Yes, I remember."

"I'd forgotten about it myself, I guess. He never talked about Silver Sands. He hadn't been here since you went away. Four years, isn't it?"

"Longer."

22

"Well, here we are," Meredith said. "Except for a few new houses it doesn't seem to have changed. But *there's* something interesting. On the beach. See them?"

At the other end of the crescent of beach two girls in bikinis were running out of the surf. One was pulling off her bathing cap and shaking out dark, smooth hair.

Rick Prentice smiled at his friend's enthusiasm. "If anything, the scenery has improved."

"Nothing like that down here in our day. Not unless we brought them with us, anyway. Notice the figure of the brunette?"

"I haven't forgotten my anatomy. But don't overlook her friend!"

Meredith chuckled as a turn in the road hid the beach and the two girls.

"Hey, hold it!" Rick exclaimed. "We've passed the gates. There's the house through the trees now."

"Been a long time," Bryan said. He braked, backed up and turned in, driving slowly.

The house seemed larger than Rick remembered. It had been built in more spacious days when redwood was abundant. Squared on three sides, the timbers had been left rounded on the outside to give it a log cabin effect. The chimney was built of rough cut stone. There had been fine flower beds once, and a couple of acres of lawn. All this had been carefully tended by the Ortez family who lived across the headland at the north end of the beach on the estuary where Dr. Henry Prentice had kept his boat.

All that was left now were rhododendrons running wild on either side of the drive.

"Well, the house still looks sound," Bryan said, studying it doubtfully as he stopped the car. "Someone has kept the drive clear, or it would have been overrun long ago. Shouldn't we drive around the Ortez place first for the key?"

"Dad always left his key on one of the porch rafters, and chances are it's still there. He used to lose keys all the time, so he always left this one here. I'll take a look."

23

A tangle of vines clogged the porch on either side, but it was clear to the front door. As he groped for the key cobwebs clung to his fingers, but he found it at last and grinned down at Bryan triumphantly.

"It's here!"

"Great." Bryan came up the steps. "Rick, this is *still* a lovely place. Don't give it up."

"I couldn't anyway. Too many memories here, Bryan. Part of Dad's life and my mother's was built into it. And part of mine too. Let's take a look inside and learn the worst."

Inside it was a lot better than he had expected. The furniture was sheathed in dust covers. The thin film of dust on shelves and walls meant that someone had been caring for the place. An hour's work would put it in order. There would be no power or light, of course. He walked over to the nearest switch and flicked it on experimentally. In the center of the large lounge the chandelier bloomed with light.

Looking up, he remembered that his mother had chosen the chandelier.

"Hey! What you do in there? You come out or I call the police!"

Someone was shouting outside. Rick went quickly to the open door and stared out. A short, burly man stood with his hands on his hips at a safe distance from the door. Behind him, Rick noticed for the first time the track through the rhododendrons leading away through the rambling grounds toward the inlet and the wharf. A stout woman stood firmly in the path surrounded by children of various ages.

Rick laughed delightedly. "Buenos tardes, Pedro! Don't you know me any more?"

The man stared up at him, suddenly his face broke into a jubilant smile. "Isabella!" he shouted. "It is the young Doc! The Señor Ricardo!"

"Oh, no! And the house the way she is!"

Her big arms brushed the children away, and Isabella Ortez rushed into the house. The children, left alone, stood huddled together watching as Pedro ran to shake Rick's hand.

"All this time and the house and the sea she is here, yet Doc Henry, he does not come. Then he dies and we are bereft, and you do not come either, *patron*. All the time we hope, so Isabella she keep the house tidy, and I look after the boat."

Rick laughed and patted his shoulder. "Pedro, I went through his accounts and couldn't find anything about you. I had no idea you were still looking after the place. I wasn't even sure it still stood. I thought he might have sold the boat."

"He would never sell the *Tern*, Señor," Pedro said, shocked. "The motors they are old now. But they still run. And the paint she is cheap paint, but the *Tern* is clean, as you will see. As the house is clean. It seemed the least we could do, Isabella and I."

Rick frowned. "And the light and power still on. Pedro, has anyone been paying you for all this?"

He shrugged. "It is not a matter of payment, Señor. It is a matter of repayment. Of something that we owe and are glad to pay. We heard that the *patron* had trouble at the hospital. People said there was not enough money to do the things that he wished to do for others, as he always has done. They said too that he had grown old and ill. Should one trouble him for such little things? He would not take money when he saved my Isabella's life. Nor when he brought two of my sons into the world. So we kept the house and the boat ready for his use, or yours. Only he never came."

"You are a good friend, Pedro," Rick said slowly. The Ortez's were poor, but they had pride. Pedro would be hurt if Rick offered him money now. But in a family that must count its pennies he knew that the cost of paint, oil and fuel for the cruiser, and electricity for the house meant real sacrifice. He would see that they did not lose by their generosity.

"Come," he said. "Someone else you know is here, Pedro. Dr. Meredith."

He could relax here, Rick Prentice decided as he went into the house with Ortez.

Beyond the northern headland of Silver Sands Beach was an estuary. Here, past the tiny, curving islet the natives called Tern Isle, a dozen houses had been built. City families had bought the new houses because of the safe swimming in Tern Bay and the convenience of mooring their boats at the Ortez wharf higher up the inlet.

In one of these houses facing the glistening water and the isle, Michelle Lambert and Carla were staring out the window at a full moon rising slowly from the sea behind Tern Bay.

"It could be a night in Tahiti," Michelle said quietly as she watched the moon etch the graceful shape of palm trees above the low island of sand.

"Those aren't coconut palms you see out there. They're palmettos. But the effect is the same. Like it?"

"Oh yes!"

"What would you like to do? There's TV, or we could spin some records on the stereo. Or if that's too much like what we do nights at the Nurses' Home, we could either take a walk to the wharf to look at Dad's boat or go for a moonlight swim in the lagoon. It's your decision."

Michelle laughed. "Let's go out. I'd like to see your dad's boat, but the moonlight swim sounds tempting too. I'll leave the decision to you, Carla."

"Then we'll do both," Carla laughed. "Come on, this is no night to stay home."

They walked along the sand of the beach, with the still water inside the lagoon stirring lazily as tiny ripples lapped the sand. The moon had not yet cleared the feathery tops of the palmettos, but it was painting a silvery trail across the water to them.

They left the houses behind and headed for the single light far along the beach that revealed a long wharf with white painted cruisers moored alongside.

"I'd take you out to sea tomorrow if Dad was here,"

26

Carla said. "But the tides are tricky, and Dad only lets me run it when he's aboard. I'd like you to see the cruiser though. It's Dad's pride and joy. And you'll be coming out with us one day. I'll see to that."

"I've never done anything like that," Michelle laughed. "But I'd love to."

"You'll probably be seasick first time out; I was. But once you get used to the motion, it's great. Hey! There's a light in the old house on the hill. See it? It's the first time since we've been coming here. You wonder why people neglect a house like that. It has the best view in the area and it must have had a fine garden once. Mother and I pick a few flowers up there every now and then. Nobody seems to bother what you do there, and the flowers go to waste anyway."

"Maybe they're too busy to come down here."

"Dad thinks it's probably part of an estate. I've meant to ask Pedro Ortez about it. The Ortez family have lived here for generations. They should know who owns it, and why it's never used."

Michelle laughed nervously. "Among all those trees it looks like a house from one of those books you're always reading."

"Well, if they neglect it much longer it might make a fine place for a coven of witches to throw a ball. There's the path we use when we go to get flowers. See it?"

It looked like a dark tunnel through the undergrowth to Michelle, and both girls instinctively began to hurry past it.

"Michelle, *what's that*?" Carla gripped her arm suddenly. Far back along the path through the bushes light began to dance on the leaves that pressed in on either side. They heard quiet voices.

"Heavens!" Michelle gasped. "Carla, don't *do* things like that! It's just people coming down the track with a flashlight. Two men, I think."

"Well, it startled me! Come on. It's dark here. I guess it's just whoever is staying at the old house."

"We should be looking at the water," Michelle murmured. "It's beautiful."

It was silent except for the rustle of sand beneath their feet. The Ortez house was just ahead now, with the wharf beyond. Someone inside the house was strumming a guitar, and Michelle could hear voices speaking Spanish.

She looked back and saw the two men coming out from the path onto the beach. The flashlight shone briefly on a man's legs, swept curiously down the beach to examine the sea, and flicked off.

"Maybe they have a boat too," Michelle said.

"They're coming this way?"

"Uh-huh. And they can probably see us against the light on the wharf."

"Well, if they're going to one of the boats we'll see them from the cabin windows."

The boats moored along the wharf in a neat row reminded Michelle of the fishing boats at Fisherman's Wharf.

"This one is Dad's," Carla said. "It's fast, and very safe at sea. Come aboard."

It looked sleek and expensive to Michelle. The name *Flying Fish* was painted in black letters on the stern. It dipped as she stepped down cautiously onto the deck, but it was quite large, and certainly luxurious.

A door slid back and light flooded the cabin. Above a carpeted floor the woodwork had a rich, clean look.

"I'll show you around and then we'll have a drink," Carla said, smiling with justifiable pride. "It's Dad's one real luxury, and he's earned it. It sleeps six, and as boats go it's quite roomy and comfortable. Come on, I'll show you. There's the galley where Mother or I cook."

After the tour Carla made two long cool drinks, and they sat on the cushioned seats and sipped them slowly, chatting and listening to the soft water sounds beyond the cabin. The drinks brought a warm, friendly glow, a feeling of companionship and well-being. Hospital routine seemed far away and unimportant. This was the right kind of relaxation, away from the often tense atmosphere of operating rooms.

28

"Like another drink?"

"No, that one was just right. Something I needed without realizing it, I guess."

"I'm glad you came with me, Michelle," Carla smiled. "We're good for each other. We must do this again. Still feel like that moonlight swim?"

"Oh yes!"

"I'll bring a flashlight from the locker. If we swim in front of the house, we won't get a chill. We'll have some nice hot coffee afterwards. Then to bed, with the sun and surf waiting again bright and early in the morning. Sound okay?"

"Sounds perfect," Michelle sighed.

"Male company is about the only thing I can think of that might improve it," Carla laughed. "Provided they were young, handsome, entertaining *and* manageable. Still, we can't have everything, can we? Which reminds me. I forgot about those two men. Did you hear them on the wharf?"

Michelle had forgotten them too. She frowned. "No, I didn't. Do you suppose they stopped at the Ortez house?"

"Maybe. Or they've gone fishing higher up the estuary. Anyway, let's go."

The two girls wandered slowly back along the moonlit beach. They left their beach coats on the sand in front of Carla's house and ran laughing into the water. It was warmer than Michelle expected and once they were in it was really pleasant; they swam slowly together, side by side.

"Let's swim out to the island."

Michelle stared across the water, frowning. "It seems a long way." She hesitated. "Do you think we should?"

"Yes. It's all right. We're over the channel now. Can't you feel it? That's why we have to tread water. But the sand starts again not far out. We can stand up any time we get tired and wade."

"Okay."

Michelle felt better when she found the firm sandy bottom with her toes.

Carla had drawn away from her slightly, swimming with long, slow strokes. As she swam to catch up, Michelle's arms and legs began to feel heavy; she gasped and felt for the bottom. She began to wade and realized that wading was just as tiring.

"You okay?" Carla called back.

"Yes. I'm wading!"

"I can hear you. Sounds like a school of hippopotamuses wallowing back there! Take it easy. Move slower and you'll find it easier. Here, grab my hand. I'm standing on a sandbar now, and it's only waist deep. Up!"

Carla dragged at her, pulling her up onto the bank. Michelle straightened, relieved, feeling the cool night air on her upper body.

"Not far now. We can rest up before we go back," Carla said reassuringly. "Say, you're really beat, aren't you? I didn't realize. Going back we'll wade out close to the channel and then all we have to do is swim across."

"I'll be okay in a minute," Michelle gasped. "It's just that I haven't swum as much as I have today in a long time."

"I should have thought of that," Carla said apologetically. "But it's okay. Nothing to worry about."

When they reached the sandy shore, Michelle stumbled up out of the water slowly, breathing hard, and sank down gratefully on dry sand. Out here the palmettos that had looked so soft and feathery against the moon earlier were stiff and rustled with a brittle sound in the night breeze. Driftwood had piled against them and beyond Tern Isle the water had a different sound. Surf pounded in there from the open sea. The breakers had a sullen sound and she could see the froth of white water out there in the moonlight.

Michelle lay on the sand and took deep breaths to end her exhaustion.

"There's someone here!" Carla gasped, gripping her arm. "Look! Coming along the isle."

They both stared at the approaching, shadowy figures.

30

"Carla, maybe it's those two men."

"Yes! They must have left their clothes near the path and swum out to the other end of the island," Carla said nervously.

Suddenly the narrow isle seemed a lonely and desolate place and the two men approaching them loomed large and frightening.

"Let's get out of here," Michelle whispered.

"Do you feel strong enough?"

"I'll make it."

"Hello there!" a masculine voice called. "That's quite a swim across. Are you girls okay?"

Carla tugged at Michelle's arm. *"Come on!"*

They went in together, waded quickly to the edge of the sandspit, leaned forward and began to swim.

"Hey there!" the voice called after them. "Better watch out! It's a flood tide. You'll find the run a lot stronger going back. Why don't you just rest up here with us? We could swim back together. We're waiting for the flat water at the top of the tide. It's easier then."

"Don't answer," Carla panted.

Michelle could not have answered if she wanted to. She managed to gasp, "Carla, let's wade a while."

"Heavens, I forgot how tired you are! Okay, We'll rest. It isn't deep here, and they can't see us."

It was deep, though; Michelle, the smaller of the two, could barely stand. The water came up to her shoulders and kept trying to lift her off her feet.

Carla's hands caught her, steadying her. "You okay?" Carla whispered anxiously. "We must've swum farther than I thought. Anyway, that means we don't have so far to swim from here."

Michelle was not so sure of that as she stared across the water at the distant light outside the beach house. It seemed miles away still, and her heart began a frightened thumping.

"They're not exactly sociable, are they?" a voice behind them said. "And I can't hear them out there, can you?"

"No. Hey girls! Why don't you be sensible and come

31

back? It can be dangerous in that channel just before the tide changes."

Michelle's mouth and nose went under unexpectedly, and she grabbed for Carla.

"Carla maybe . . . the tide is rising fast, and . . ." she gasped.

"No. We just swam farther out than I thought. Take no notice. They're just trying to lure us back there. The key's a lonely place. Like being on a desert island almost at this time of night."

"Can you hear them?" one of the men asked. His voice carried clearly across the water.

"No. I'm beginning to think we imagined them."

"Like mermaids?"

"Then they can probably swim like fish, and they have a start, not much chance of catching them."

"Let's try anyway. They're not swimming, so they can't be far away."

The two girls turned their heads in fear. Staring back they watched the two shadows move silently into the water.

"Come on!" Carla hissed. "I'll stay close. If you feel tired turn on your back and rest. I'll tow you."

The water lifted Michelle, and she had difficulty getting her feet up to kick. She kicked noisily for a moment before she stretched out beside Carla.

The two men stopped abruptly.

"Hear that? There they are! Swimming now. To the left."

"Come on!"

Michelle could hardly control her desire to thrash away as fast as she could. She tried to swim slowly and conserve her strength. She kept assuring herself that the two men back there were concerned only with their safety, but she wasn't convinced.

The heavy feeling came back into her arms and legs worse than before. She could barely lift them.

"Carla!" she gasped. "I'll have . . . to rest . . . !"

"I'm here," Carla panted.

She felt Carla's hands as she turned over. Beneath

32

her, Carla's legs kicked sturdily, creating swirling phosphorescence. They seemed to be making little headway. She could see the palmettos on Tern Isle and they seemed to be drifting rapidly in the opposite direction. She could see something else, too. The flailing action of their arms as the two men swam steadily after them, side by side.

Carla gasped suddenly. "Michelle," she panted. "I've never . . . seen the current . . . like this before! I don't seem able to get out of . . . the channel. We'll have to go with it! You must help me! Try to . . . kick."

Michelle tried, but now the palmettos seemed to be moving faster. Carla had turned with her, going with the current and she could see the light outside the beach house receding rapidly.

Michelle closed her eyes, feeling sick suddenly. She was going to drown, she decided, out here in the darkness. They were both going to drown. Only she couldn't let Carla drown with her. Carla could reach the beach.

"Carla, leave me, and swim ashore!" she gasped. "I'll be . . . all right. I can . . . still float, tread water. I'm not so tired now. Get help at the . . . Ortez house."

"No! No, I won't. We're almost on the bar at the end of the lagoon. There's . . . rough water here."

"I'll be all right!" Her fear for Carla gave her strength, and she thrust away from her, turning over. She began to swim feebly away, hearing Carla's anguished cry as she came after her.

"No, Michelle! *Don't* . . . !"

Suddenly a wave lifted her. A second slapped her in the face, engulfing her. The water seized her, sucking her down. She felt herself turning, rolling about beneath the water. Sand grazed the length of her body and with her breath spent she thrust up instinctively from the bottom, gasping for air.

She glimpsed the moon and flailing arms.

"There she is!" Carla screamed.

The water sucked her under again. Her lungs felt as though they were bursting. She struggled in terror. Something, some hard body rammed against her and

33

arms gripped her. She was being borne upwards swiftly. She gasped in air. Someone was turning her on her back, starting to swim with her. They were not Carla's hands gripping her now, but a man's strong hands.

"I've got her!" a voice close to her ear shouted. "Look after the other one, Bryan! Go with it. Swim toward the wharf."

She drifted then, with her arms trailing, feeling legs churning the water strongly beneath her. She bumped against something hard. The legs stopped their steady thrashing beneath her, and she realized vaguely that the white, hard shape above her was a boat, and that the light she could see was on the Ortez wharf. He was holding her with one arm now, and with the other he was clinging to a platform just above water level at the stern of the boat.

Someone was running along the wharf to help them. A young, burly man in swim trunks dripping with water. The boat bounced as he jumped down, then he was scrambling out onto the platform.

"I'll take her, Rick. How is she?"

"Waterlogged!" her rescuer panted grimly. "And no more than she deserves! Of all the fool things to do!"

He lifted her gently from the water, and the man who had saved her scrambled out of the water beside her. Carla's face peered down anxiously from the rail of the wharf.

"Let me take her," a voice said. She was lifted in someone's arms, and she felt as though she was going to be sick. Things started to blur, and her lungs hurt. Then she felt herself slide down, down, down, into darkness.

When she regained consciousness she was lying on a bunk in the cabin of Carla's boat. She could vaguely see Carla's face watching her over someone's shoulder. A man's shoulder. He was kissing her, she decided. Now he had turned his face aside and was breathing in deeply. He was kissing her again. Only why did he hold her nose pinched shut while he kissed?

She couldn't breathe this way, or return his kiss. She

began to struggle suddenly as she thought about that, and someone laughed.

"Didn't take much reviving anyway," a man's voice said. He was lifting her shoulders gently. The taste of brandy was in her mouth, and he had spilled some that she could feel running down inside the bra of her bikini. The bra seemed loose and she supposed they had undone it to help her breathing. Her hands went up instinctively to hold it in place as his voice asked gently, "How do you feel now, Michelle?"

"I'm . . . okay . . ." Her eyes opened slowly, heavy-lidded. She stared up at him.

He had gray eyes and his unruly black hair was still damp from the water.

Carla suddenly began to cry, and the other man put his arms around her to comfort her. Then she recognized him. He was not a stranger at all, but Dr. Bryan Meredith of Hillside.

Carla was sobbing something that sounded awfully foolish.

"All the time it was Bryan and Dr. Prentice we were trying to run away from, Michelle. You almost drowned because we did that. I forgot—you haven't met Dr. Prentice yet."

"But we have met, Carla," Rick said. "In about ten feet of water with the waves turning her end over end. I'm very glad we did. She's all right now. We'll take her home and put her to bed and she'll wake up in the morning just fine. Only as her doctor, I'm prescribing a quiet day fishing tomorrow in the *Tern*. That goes for you too, Carla. Dr. Meredith and I in consultation have decided to allow you both to surf a little tomorrow afternoon, but only under our supervision. Does anyone have an objection?" he asked, looking down at Michelle.

She smiled. "I think I'd like that."

chapter three

The *Tern* was neither modern or luxurious. It was a wooden boat, its furnishing plain, but it seemed freshly painted and clean. It reminded Michelle of fishing boats she had seen off the coast of Maine. Its engines thumped heavily, and it was slow in the water. It was like a comfortable old lady, Michelle thought.

"Sit tight now," Dr. Rick Prentice said as he looked up from the fishing gear he was preparing. "We're about to cross the bar. No need for anyone to be seasick on a day like this. There're always a few waves on the bar, but once we're outside you'll find the sea as calm as a lake."

Michelle laughed nervously. "I hope so, Rick."

He stood up, braced his feet and stared ahead. Studying him, Michelle decided that he was even more handsome this morning than he had seemed last night. White shorts and a short-sleeved white shirt open at the neck contrasted with his deep suntan.

He did not look like a doctor, she decided. But then, she supposed, she didn't look like a nurse in her brief shorts and blouse.

Carla looked out the door of the wheelhouse. "Don't let her fall overboard Rick!" she laughed. "She gave us enough trouble last night."

"I haven't forgotten!" Rick said. He sat down beside

her, and smiled at her. "I'm not likely to forget," he added quietly.

"I'm sorry I gave you so much trouble." She shivered and glanced at the northern end of Tern Isle which they were now passing. "You must think we're both very naive."

"We were worried about you. We both know that channel and what it can do on a flood tide. Sometimes the bar at the southern end of the lagoon washes right out, and the water runs between Tern Isle and the shore like a millrace. Afterward when Carla explained, we both realized that what we said out there might have sounded sinister to two girls alone in the dark."

They stood close together and Rick held her protectively with his arm.

"We're past the bar now," he said, smiling. "Calm water ahead."

He withdrew his arm slowly, almost reluctantly.

"Rick," Michelle said. "Last night on the *Flying Fish* I had the impression that someone was kissing me. It was the strangest feeling."

His smile, she decided, was mischievous and a little guilty. "Oh? People often dream when recovering consciousness, you know."

"Yes, I know."

"Do you know about mouth-to-mouth resuscitation?"

"Yes I do."

"That may have prompted your dream. Because that's how you were revived. But I won't say I wasn't tempted, Michelle. You were very pale, but still beautiful last night. Your lips were cold, and I wanted desperately to warm them. When they began to warm I knew you were coming to. It was a good feeling."

Carla was coming from the wheelhouse and he changed the subject. She was laughing, looking back over her shoulder at Bryan Meredith, and looking happier than Michelle had ever seen her look before.

"The helmsman wants his navigating instructions, Skipper," she laughed. "Michelle, how are you making out? No queasy feelings, I hope?"

"No. I feel fine."

"She's never fished before, Rick," Carla said, "and I'm no expert. I'm afraid you'll have to teach her. What shall I tell Bryan?"

"Tell him we'll look for tuna wide off Twin Heads. Pedro Ortez saw some schools out there through the week, feeding on pilchards. They should still be around. We'll start circling when we find them. We can all fish then, provided they're not too big for you girls to handle. I'll talk to Bryan. Stay with Michelle for a moment, will you, Carla."

"Be a pleasure to do *anything* for that man," Carla smiled as he left them alone. She looked at Michelle impishly. "Like him?"

"Yes, of course." Michelle felt herself flush. She said quickly, "If we all fish, who will drive the boat out there?"

Carla laughed. "The boat will look after itself, silly. They lash the wheel and it just goes around and around in slow circles among the school of fish. We'll be over deep water and wide out, so we can't get into any trouble. You'll like it. It's fun."

"I'm sure I will." She was beginning to like everything about today, she decided.

The boat was following the coast line south, past the headland, turning into a slight swell rolling down the coast, with the Pacific at its sparkling blue best.

"There they are!" Rick Prentice called from the wheelhouse. "Come up here and have a look, girls."

Michelle got up doubtfully. The deck beneath her feet would not keep still, and she found the motion disturbing. She gripped the rail in panic every now and then as she followed Carla, who seemed able to walk as steadily here as she would along the hospital corridors.

"What are they, Bryan?" Carla called excitedly as they went up the steps and clung to the small iron rails along the roof of the wheelhouse.

"Two schools," Bryan Meredith said. "Skipjack, and small blues. Want the glasses? Here."

"Skipjack?" Carla said, frowning at him. "What the heck are skipjack?"

"Stripies, Carla," Bryan grinned. "Where did you go to school?"

"Skipjack? Stripies? Huh!" Carla said disgustedly. "My dad calls them bonito, and I'm sure he's right. He knows his fish."

"There *is* a difference," Bryan laughed. "Maybe I'll teach him which is which one day, if his daughter will invite me for a weekend."

"His daughter might just take you up on that, Dr. Meredith," she replied. "But don't think Dad won't give you an argument. He was fishing when you were in short pants."

Michelle laughed as Bryan pulled up the window and made a wry face at her friend's back.

It was easier going back to her seat. She only lurched once and made a grab at the rail. She supposed she was getting used to the motion of the *Tern*.

Soon she could see the fish quite plainly. Gulls began to circle over the boat. The fish seemed huge to Michelle and suddenly she could see hordes of other tiny silver fish clouding the water all about the *Tern*. She laughed excitedly as about a dozen of them threw themselves up out of the water and seemed to run along on their tails.

"Time to find out what you can do," Rick Prentice said. "Sit here and face the stern. You hold the rod like this. Firmly. They're not giants, but they'll strike hard and you'll really know when you're reeling in your first."

She held the rod as he showed her, and settled into the padded seat. He began to play out line for her as the *Tern* began circling slowly through the school. Bryan came hurrying from the wheelhouse to stand beside Carla, and started doing the same thing for her.

At the end of the two receding lines Michelle could see the lures glinting in the sun on the surface of the water. A tiny mane of white water formed behind the glinting, spinning steel lure. She watched another larger

39

mane of white water appear suddenly, rushing in toward her lure from the side.

"Hang on!" Rick cried. "He's going to strike!"

Something almost tore the rod from her hands then. It bent crazily with line running out and she was fighting a threshing, plunging fish that leaped out of the water, gleaming blue in the sunshine, then jerked from side to side frantically as it tried to dislodge the hooks.

She had cried out sharply, without being aware of it. And Rick's arm was around her, holding her back in the seat.

"Hold him! You're doing fine! He's sounding now, diving right down to the bottom of the sea. If there's a reef down there, rocks that he can snag the line around you'll lose him."

"I'm not . . . going . . . to lose him!" she panted. She began to wind the reel and pump the rod instinctively, and Rick shouted delightedly near her ear, "Hey, watch this, Bryan! I'm coaching a future champion here!"

"Got a champion of my own who's doing fine," Bryan shouted. "Hey, hold him honey! *Hold* him!"

Michelle glimpsed Carla's startled blue eyes as big as saucers as she too fought a plunging fish. Her own hands seemed barely able to hold the rod, but Michelle was winding in, bringing her fish back toward the surface, despite its furious downward plunging. She was determined he wasn't going to free himself around a rock and leave her with broken, empty line.

"You've got him!" Rick said exultantly. "He's surfacing, and he's all in! Just keep winding, and I'll gaff him for you."

"There he is!" Carla screamed. "Oh! *It's a monster!*"

"That isn't yours—it's Michelle's!" Bryan laughed. "Wind, honey! Wind, or you'll lose yours!"

Rick had left her and was bending over the stern with what looked like a giant fishhook lashed to the end of a short pole.

"Oh, be careful Rick!" Michelle cried as he balanced, reaching down.

"It's okay. Got him. It's a bluefin! We've started them off on the big fellows, Bryan!"

"We're midway between the two schools," Bryan said. "That's why. They're mixed up at the edge. Carla's is a bluefin too."

Her own fish came up out of the water and fell into the boat. The rod went slack in Michelle's hands and she squealed and lifted her bare legs hurriedly as the fish thrashed about on the deck. She stared at it in mingled pride and dismay. Sleek, shaped like a torpedo, it looked huge and beautiful, all rich blues and purples shimmering in the sunlight, but it was bleeding all over the deck near her feet before Rick could disengage the hook and lift it into a huge wooden box that waited in the cockpit.

"Better than forty pounds," Rick said triumphantly. "A few more like that and we'll feed the whole hospital." He noticed Michelle's expression then. "Hey, what's the matter?"

"I made him bleed," she said. "And he's such a beautiful creature."

He laughed. "I probably did that with the gaff. And fish don't have the right kind of nervous system to feel pain, remember? He was also something of a cannibal, devouring literally thousands of those poor little pilchards out there. His color will fade now that you've caught him. In a few minutes he'll look just like any other fish, except larger."

"You're just saying that."

"No, it's the truth. And we're fishing for food today as well as sport, which makes the spilling of a little tuna blood permissible."

He turned back to gaff Carla's fish. She watched Carla's excitement as it came aboard, and Carla's dismay as it bled much more than hers.

After that the men took over while they both watched. The big fish came in steadily, as alike as peas in size and color. The girls watched for a while, then moved in to the cabin to prepare lunch while the men

41

filled the huge box, packed it with ice and then slid it below.

Lunch was a gay affair, and the sea had given them an appetite. The schools of tuna had moved farther north by then, but the men set lines from the deck. The fish they caught that way were smaller, but added to the variety with white sea bass and reef fish.

After lunch the men hauled up the anchor and the *Tern* headed for home, with everyone already thinking of the waiting surf at Silver Sands.

Carla and Bryan sat close together in the stern, trailing a forgotten line for stray bonito.

"Would you like to take the wheel?" Rick asked Michelle. "It's quite simple. You hold it like this, and the boat steers like a car. Swing the wheel to the left or the right and that's the way she goes. Try it."

She tried it, aware of his closeness and the way he touched her, placing her hands on the wheel. It seemed simple, as he said. She experimented a little, easing the wheel first one way then the other. She looked back at him, smiling.

"How am I doing, Captain?"

"As you did with the tuna, Michelle. Perfectly. I'm beginning to think that's the way you are. Perfect." He said it gravely, but with a smile.

They were silent for a while and then Rick said hesitantly, "Michelle?"

"Yes, Rick?"

"Why did you leave all your friends and come so far away from home, leave Bellevue and the great Dr. Henderson to come to Hillside?"

She stared ahead over the calm sea. "That's important, Rick?"

"To me . . ."

She said slowly: "I wanted to forget something. Something that happened. It wasn't possible there. There was too much to remind me of it."

"Something—or someone?" he asked.

"Someone," she said. "We were very close. We only had each other. He was a Navy pilot. He was shot down

42

over North Vietnam. The report said missing, presumed dead. You should know about such things. It's harder when you can't be sure. I kept hoping." She stopped speaking and then added quietly. "I broke down, waiting. It was Dr. Henderson who suggested I should come here. He helped me get the job at Hillside. He knew your father."

So that was it! He studied the back of her head in dismay. The poor kid!

"I'm sorry Michelle. I wish I hadn't brought this up."

"No. I'd like to talk to you about it, Rick," she said slowly. "You were out there, weren't you? What do you think? They said he wasn't far in over North Vietnam. He *could* have parachuted to safety."

She wanted him to verify that, he knew. Or to say that the guy had probably been taken prisoner.

He said slowly, "Usually when a flier has to bale out he's in close touch with the rest of his squadron. Someone reports in to control at once and they get him out if they can. We don't lose any men it's possible to save. When did it happen?"

"Last April, Rick. The fourteenth, at six in the morning, they said."

April? He had been in Vietnam in April. He remembered seeing men brought in, some of them unidentifiable. He felt a need to know the man's name, but was reluctant to ask.

He said, "Sometimes when a flier bales out over the jungle he hides out in there and finds his own way back. That can take a long time."

"Yes," she said. "I thought that. They knew he was in trouble and was going down, but nobody saw him. There were clouds they said. They didn't *know*. He just said that the plane had been hit and he was going down. After that, nothing. But if he wasn't wounded, he must have been able to use his parachute?" She was silent then for a few moments. "Is it so terrible, if he has been taken prisoner, Rick?" she asked quietly.

"They're trained for it. They know what to expect and they can take it," he said. "If he's a prisoner, he has a chance of getting back home some day. But when you're dead, there's none. If a man is missing, our people keep after it until they know what happened," he said, feeling a need to explain, to reassure despite his conviction that the man was dead, that he had never been taken prisoner. "But sooner or later they find out. You can be sure of that, Michelle. They'll question people on the ground, try to piece it together. If it would help, I still have friends there. I could write to someone who may be able to give you information quicker than you'd receive it through the official channels. Would you like me to try?"

"Would you, Rick? Please." She turned her head quickly to look him and he realized for the first time that she was crying, that she must have been crying silently all the time.

"Okay," he said gruffly. "I'll do that."

He went down into the cabin and came back with a notebook.

"Perhaps you'd better write down a few details while I take the wheel."

He stared out over the sea ahead while she wrote. "Do you know his next of kin?" he asked without looking around.

"I thought I told you. I am."

"Then write that down," he said.

She scribbled obediently and handed him back the notebook and ballpoint, putting her hand on the wheel as he took them and glanced at what she had written.

"Thanks. This should do it. If . . ." he broke off abruptly. "Lieutenant James Carson Lambert?"

"Yes, that's right."

"His name is the same as yours? You're his wife?"

She shook her head. "No, of course not, Rick. Jim and I are brother and sister. Neither of us had time to fall in love with anyone or think about marriage. We were both too busy trying to graduate, and afterwards I went to Bellevue and Jim to San Diego. I told you how close we've always been. I suppose that was because there were only the three of us, Mother, Jim and I, after my father was killed in Korea. Dad was a major in the Marines. Major Carson Lambert. He won a citation. That was why Jim went to Naval College. When Mother died a year ago that left just the two of us."

And now you're alone, he thought, studying her over the notebook. The thought brought a strange tenderness, that came into his eyes involuntarily.

She looked away uncertainly. "Was there anything else you needed to know?"

"No," he said.

"When you said that you looked as though . . ." she broke off. "I thought something was wrong. That I'd offended you in some way. I wouldn't want to do that, Rick. Not after last night, and what you're trying to do for me now. You'd like Jim, and I'm sure Jim would like you. Are you sure I haven't said anything to annoy you? Nothing is wrong, is it Rick?"

He smiled. "Of course not, Michelle."

"You're so kind," she said. "I want to thank you."

It was meant to be a kiss of gratitude, but it didn't feel that way at all. And afterward when she thought about it she could not be sure whether she had instigated it or he had. It left her breathless and trembling. One thing she knew; she would long remember it.

He would have kissed her again, she knew, only the *Tern* started to buck and swing around.

"Hey there! Watch it!" Bryan Meredith called anxiously.

They were almost on the bar Michelle discovered, as her eyes opened. Rick took the wheel in his hands again, laughing apologetically.

"Say, what's the matter with you in there?" Bryan called indignantly.

"Not a thing, Bryan! Everything's fine!" Rick called back.

They began to pass Tern Isle again, still sparkling in the sunlight. Soon they would be surfing together.

This was, she decided, the most wonderful day of her life.

chapter four

Carla drove well, but this morning the traffic along the Coastal Highway was thick and frustrating, and she was wishing secretly that they'd driven back last night after dinner when Bryan and Rick Prentice had left Silver Sands. Carla drove silently, with the traffic taking all her concentration. As they approached the city they realized that they were going to cut it close at Hillside, with barely time to change into uniform and run across to the hospital and the operating rooms. Michelle was silent too. She was remembering the lingering kiss Rick had given her when he left her outside the cottage the night before.

"Oh damn!" Carla said loudly. "Someone must have stopped on the road! The traffic's just crawling."

The cars and trucks were bumper to bumper for two miles. Ahead a siren wailed thinly as the traffic ground almost to a standstill.

"Well, at least both surgeons will know where we are," Michelle said, smiling.

Carla laughed. "It's Miss Pringle I'm thinking about, not the surgeons. That's Sam's ambulance. I'd bet on it. The siren's sort of falsetto, and southern approaches are in our area for road accidents."

"I hadn't thought of that, that it could be a surgical

emergency," Michelle said in dismay, "and we're late already. Miss Pringle will have plenty to say."

The delay proved shorter than Carla expected, however. Police began waving cars past the accident. A car and truck were locked together, and another smaller car had turned sideways across the traffic line, bumped there as the other vehicles had met almost head-on.

An ambulance stood beside the wreckage, and turning her head as Carla drove past, Michelle recognized the fair-haired intern bending over someone on a stretcher near the crashed car.

"You were right, it was our ambulance. Dr. Moreton was attending to someone. It looked like a head-on collision between a big car and a truck. Another car was involved, the small car you had to drive around. The big car was a Cadillac. I think the two people in it were hurt. One was a woman."

"VIPs," Carla said disgustedly. "They think everyone else has to give way to them!"

"It could have been the truck. I noticed one of the front wheels off. It could have swerved into the wrong lane."

"Well, the hospital grapevine will have all the gory details no doubt," Carla said. "It seldom misses. We're not going to be all that late now."

Their luck had changed. The traffic opened out and Carla turned into the drive outside the Hillside Nurses' Home with the thin wail of the ambulance still far behind them.

It became a race between the two girls and they both freshened up and changed into uniform in record time, hearing the stragglers of the shift going down in the elevator as they gave the final touches to starched uniforms and caps, with Carla beating Michelle to the door by inches.

Miss Marsden, supervising nurse of O.R. looked up angrily as the two girls hurried in together.

"Oh there you are! At last! I expected you both in earlier this morning. After all, it's Dr. Prentice's first operation here since his return; nothing spectacular, just a gall, but there's a femoral artery embolectomy later in the day. One of Dr. Creighton's patients. They haven't decided the time yet. I want everything exactly right for him, and no slip-ups. Here are your lists. I'm sure I don't know why you couldn't have been early this morning."

"Honestly!" Carla said as Miss Marsden bustled away. "Maybe we should have told her how lucky she is we're here at all right now."

They went through to the annex where Carla, whose duties were different, left her friend. Michelle went to work smoothly and efficiently. This morning though, she found herself listening for a familiar brisk footstep, and she thought ahead uncertainly to their first meeting here. A meeting that must be different from the easy camaraderie of yesterday.

As though her thoughts had produced him, Rick Prentice came in at that moment with Carl Myers, Hillside's highly skilled anesthetist. Dr. Myers, a gray-haired stocky man in his fifties, with startling blue eyes, called all the nurses by their first names, a practice that Dr. Henry Prentice had frowned upon. Only the conscientious Miss Marsden had rated *that* in Dr. Henry's opinion.

Dr. Myers said cheerfully, "Good morning, Michelle. Have a good weekend?"

"Wonderful, Doctor." She avoided looking at Rick, who was smiling at her from beside him.

"What time is Mrs. Simpson's gall?"

"It's scheduled for nine, Doctor."

"Oh, nine is it? Then we're early. Have you two met? Rick, this is Michelle Lambert. Attractive, isn't she? She is also a very good scrub nurse, believe it or not. And as you've probably discovered long ago, a good scrub nurse is the surgeon's third hand. At least your father always said so."

"Miss Lambert and I have met," Rick said, smiling at her gravely, but with his gray eyes twinkling. "Good morning, Michelle. Is Kay inside?"

He had made it easy for her, and she was grateful.

"Good morning, Dr. Prentice," she said managing to smile again. "Miss Marsden is inside preparing."

"Thank you." His eyes lingered briefly, holding hers before he walked away. "I'll look at the X-rays first, Carl," he said to Myers. "Then I'd like to discuss the anesthesia with you. Mrs. Simpson's age and arteries might make this one a little difficult."

"Oh Doctor!" Carla called to him, holding the phone in her hand. "Dr. Prentice!"

He turned at once, recognized Carla and smiled. "Yes, what is it, Carla?"

"Dr. Creighton is calling from Casualty. He has a new admission he wants to talk to you about."

He came back briskly, and Myers went through into the operating room. As she worked, Michelle watched him. He was making notes on a pad as he talked.

"Depressed fracture of the skull . . . temporoparietal area. Yes . . . Notice any nervous tic or facial twitching? Which side? The left? I see. Sounds like pressure on the brain, doesn't it? We'll have to relieve that quickly. Yes. Well, let's put it this way, George. It sounds as though pressure either from the indented bone at the point of fracture, or from a massive blood clot is building up in there, and the vessel is still hemorrhaging. Have the relatives been contacted? I'll want to talk to her next of kin after we've discussed it. Better start Pathology working on her blood group, and have her X-rayed as quickly as possible. We may have to operate as soon as we've seen the X-rays. No. If necessary we'll postpone Mrs. Simpson's gall. I'll talk to Kay Marsden about that and be right down."

He put down the phone and went into the operating room frowning with concentration. Absorbed by his problem he had forgotten Michelle.

Kay Marsden came out almost at once, with an exasperated expression on her face.

"Hold everything!" she said. "There could be a change in schedule. Emergency brain surgery instead of the gall. A probable trephine. Better start checking the sterilizer lists, Michelle. Try to cover every eventuality.

I'll give you the list as soon as possible. I want you to scrub in as soon as you're sure everything the surgeons may need is available and sterile. We'll be ready then for whichever operation Dr. Prentice decides to take first. Today of all days, and nothing going smoothly! Well, whatever happens we'll let Dr. Prentice see what we can do in O.R. Dr. Henry always said we were the best surgical team in this city, and that's the way we're going to keep it."

"Yes, Miss Marsden."

"Even if some fool socialite charges a heavy truck head-on and throws our whole schedule out for the day, we mustn't allow it to upset us, must we?"

"No, Miss Marsden. Did you say a socialite? We saw a car involved in an accident on the road this morning, driving up from Carla's beach house."

Kay Marsden glanced at her sharply. "So that's why you weren't in early this morning?"

"Yes. The traffic was held up. They had someone on a stretcher. A woman."

"That's her," Kay Marsden said with obvious disgust. "Her name is Bernice Randolf. She's well known. Owns a shipping line, and a few other items, like some oil wells and mines and such. Lives with an aunt over in St. Francis Wood, and makes the social columns every week."

Carla had crossed to them and was listening with interest. "Not *that* Bernice Randolf? Wow! No woman has any right to look the way she does and have all that money too."

"I thought she must be old," Michelle said, "when you said she ran a shipping company."

"She's about twenty-five and looks like a film star," Carla said excitedly. "And she doesn't run anything, it's all inherited from her parents. She just works full time at spending it, but I'll bet she never catches up, even with three or four broken engagements behind her, and a lot of law suits that cost plenty. She's the princess of playgirls in these parts, Michelle."

"A playgirl with a fractured skull," Kay Marsden

said grimly. "I doubt that Miss Randolf will be doing much playing for some time." She bustled away importantly.

"I wonder who Bernice Randolf's doctor is?" Carla said when Kay had left them alone together in the annex. "Probably Dr. Mervyn Stone."

"Dr. Stone? Do I know him? Is he one of our attendings?"

"Who? Mervyn Stone? You're joking, honey!" Carla laughed. "Mervyn is one of the leading doctors in this city. Socially, anyway. Nothing on his books under the millionaire class. And he's going to throw a fit when he discovers dear Bernice has been brought to Hillside."

"Why so?" Michelle asked indignantly. "Hillside is as good as they come."

"Except that Mervyn doesn't have an interest in Hillside. He'd prefer her to be taken to a hospital of his choosing, naturally. He'd want consultations with leading specialists and surgeons of his choosing too before anyone lifted a scalpel, and all that at diamond-studded fees.'"

"If he did, he could have a dead patient," Michelle said hotly. "A massive brain hemorrhage isn't going to wait for interminable consultations; or specialists to be flown in."

"Well, maybe Mervyn wouldn't go quite that far," Carla admitted. "But there'd be a long and profitable convalescence, and the fees would be enormous. I worked in one of his hospitals, and believe me, he's only in medicine for one thing: what Mervyn Stone can get out of it."

There were doctors like that, Michelle knew. But fortunately they were few. Just as there were neurotic people among the wealthy—and not only among the wealthy—who liked the attention that doctors like Mervyn Stone were willing to give them at a price.

Of one thing she was sure though. Wherever she had been taken, Bernice Randolf would not have found more efficient hospitalization or surgery than she would receive at Hillside.

She began scrubbing rhythmically; palms, nails, backs of hands, forearms, squirting the antiseptic on the brush and into the palm of her left hand, and scrub, scrub, scrubbing the tingling skin. She no longer needed the timer, but she always set it just the same and checked it against her own instinctive timing.

Kay Marsden looked in anxiously as she worked on the back of her right hand.

"Michelle, it's the trephine first. The surgeons are coming up now. Dr. Creighton is assisting Dr. Prentice. I have the list here, and you've covered it with your sterilizing. Can you be set up by the time Dr. Prentice has scrubbed?"

"Quite easily, Miss Marsden."

"Good! I was depending on you. I was talking to Lisa Grahame, who was Dr. Henry's scrub nurse before you came. She says Dr. Rick Prentice likes to feel the instrument in his palm when you pass it to him. So pass firmly, will you? I want everything to run smoothly for him."

"So do I, Miss Marsden. I'll remember."

"He likes medium blades, and asked for three sizes in polyethylene tubing. It's on the list."

"I have them soaking, Miss Marsden."

"Good girl! Sometimes I wish the others were as co-operative as you."

"They are."

"Well, maybe. Some of the time. Don't be any longer than you can help now, will you?"

"Not a moment longer, Miss Marsden."

Poor old Kay, she thought, smiling secretly. You're really in a spin this morning! And so would I be I suppose, except that we met yesterday, and I know that he isn't frightening, or bad tempered, or domineering, as so many of them are. He's really very nice. A little jealous maybe, if he happens to like you. And maybe he could be possessive, if he thought he really owned you. But in the O.R. he's going to be calm and gentle and considerate to everyone on the team.

Or maybe I'm prejudiced, she thought, because of

52

what he's trying to do about Jim. And maybe too, because as a man, not as a doctor, I like him even more than he seems to like me.

The operating room was ready and everyone was waiting for the arrival of the surgeons.

"Was Dr. Prentice scrubbing when you came in, Des?" asked Kay.

The resident, Dr. Richardson grinned behind his mask. "Yes. But someone came in. A doctor. He said his name was Stone, and this was his patient. I'm not sure, but I think he wanted to move Miss Randolf to another hospital. Dr. Prentice and Dr. Creighton were discussing it with him when I left."

"Heatedly?" Myers, the anesthetist asked, with interest.

"Dr. Stone appeared to be the heated one," Richardson said, "and the loser. Dr. Prentice seems to have acquired the habit of command in the army."

Myers chuckled. "I would like to have seen that! Where's Stone now, I wonder?"

"Something was said about X-rays. He's probably studying them."

"And that's evidence Mervyn Stone can't deny, so we may be having a hostile observer in here," Myers said. "Even Mervyn wouldn't be fool enough to take his patient away from here after seeing the X-rays."

Richardson gave him a warning look. The surgeons were coming in, followed by a man Michelle had not seen before. He was masked, capped and gowned, but wearing no gloves. A short, round-faced man with angry blue eyes narrowed above his mask.

Rick's eyes were cold. He walked straight to the operating table and took his place there, with Dr. Creighton moving in beside Richardson.

"How is she, Carl?" Rick asked the anesthetist.

"Her pulse is 100, Doctor. Her pressure 110 over 70. Respiration satisfactory."

"Good." He was looking around, checking meticulously while Kay called for an observation stool for

Dr. Stone. Rick ordered the coagulator brought in closer to Richardson. He checked the intravenous tubes.

"Everyone ready? Good. Then let's go. Knife, Miss Lambert."

Momentarily Rick's eyes met Michelle's as she passed the scalpel, they warmed, and she knew that he was smiling at her behind his mask. Then he bent over to study the operative area. He entered a world of his own, where she could only observe him and respond automatically to his needs. She watched him put pressure on the scalpel, swinging it in a smooth circle around the bruised and indented area of the fracture. Watching the edges of skin part, and the first red seepage of blood, Michelle concentrated upon her own task.

With the primary incision clamped, the scalpel cut deeper, exposing damaged bone. Then Rick began to bore the first hole through the bone. A number of these holes would circle the fracture and be joined in a single circular cut with a thin, flexible saw passed in through one hole and drawn through another.

Watching him, Michelle decided that he was a fine surgeon. He had a certainty of purpose and worked without waste of motion or loss of concentration.

Michelle glanced at Dr. Stone. His legs seemed too short for the high stool needed to give him a view of the surgeon and patient. He was obviously still very angry, but he was leaning forward now, becoming interested as a doctor, despite his personal feelings.

Rick had straightened, and she watched him withdraw the saw. He glanced over at Stone.

"We're about to remove the depressed area of bone, Dr. Stone," he said. "Would you like to move in closer?"

Stone shook his head.

"As you wish."

Rick bent again. "Ready, George?"

Creighton began lifting the circle of bone on his side with infinite care. He stopped. "Something catching under here, Doctor. Feels like a sliver of bone near the center of the fracture caught in the dura."

54

"Try drawing it gently toward you."

Creighton tried, shook his head.

"Then it's one on this side, slanting down toward you. Let me try."

Rick bent again, easing the circle of bone up and toward himself, the forceps gripping its edge through one of the burr holes.

"Got it," Creighton's voice said, relieved.

The two surgeons looked down at the dura mater, the tough protective membrane that covered the brain. Michelle could see that a sliver of bone had torn the dura mater. It was discolored there, and bulged from the pressure of a hematoma inside. She knew that somewhere within that sheath of gray membrane the brain itself had probably been pierced. A vessel, perhaps only a small and unimportant one, had been torn or severed, and was now seeping blood. Blood that would kill unless it was removed and the seepage stopped.

"You're going to have to go in, Rick," Creighton said in a grim voice.

Rick nodded. "Dr. Stone, would you mind moving in closer?" he asked. "A sliver of bone at the point of fracture has penetrated the brain. I propose to evacuate the clot by suction. We'll then attempt to seal off the bleeder by electrosurgery. But I'd like your opinion."

Stone was climbing down reluctantly from his stool, his eyes apprehensive as he came edging forward to peer down from behind Rick. He had become unaccustomed to the sight of major surgery, Michelle decided. His eyes turned sick, and he backed away.

"Well, Doctor?" Rick asked calmly.

"I agree, of course," Stone muttered behind his mask. His voice steadied and raised. Michelle knew that he was saying it to all of them, protecting himself by a statement in front of witnesses. "It is more serious than I thought at first, which is understandable, I think, since I was given no adequate time for observation or diagnosis."

"We had you called as soon as she was admitted,

Doctor," Creighton said coldly. "It was unfortunate that you took so long to get here, but since you see the urgency now I'm sure you must agree with the necessity for an emergency operation on your patient?"

"The evidence is there *now*," Stone said.

"Evidence was already there in the X-rays," Creighton said disgustedly. "As both Dr. Prentice and I pointed out to you."

"I've never doubted your ability, or Dr. Prentice's," Stone said defensively. "I doubted that you had the facilities for such an operation here at Hillside. That was all. I thought then, and I still think, she would have been better off at St. Clair. However, since the urgency is now beyond doubt I'm convinced that I am doing what is best for my patient by agreeing to what has been done here, and what you are about to attempt. My patient's welfare is the principal, indeed the only consideration, with me."

"I'm sure it is, Doctor," Creighton said sarcastically. Stone went back to his stool.

"How is she now, Carl?" Rick asked in a low voice.

"Pressure's improved slightly," Myers said. "Pulse stronger, but still 100. Pressure has improved to 120 over 80. You must have relieved some of the pressure in there when you removed the fractured segment of bone."

"Good."

Rick bent again. On the dura mater the small veins showed clearly in a tree-like pattern as George Creighton swabbed the area carefully with saline. They studied it closely together.

"We'll coagulate these first," Rick said quietly. "Ready, Dr. Richardson?"

The resident surgeon moved in with the electrode of the coagulator. Rick took it, touching it carefully to the tiny veins on each side of that small, ragged tear in the membrane while Richardson worked the current. Under the hissing impact the veins turned black as the blood within them coagulated, sealing them off one by one.

Across the operating table Michelle heard Creighton

56

sigh in relief. No blood would flow from those veins now when the surgeon cut. She had the slender-bladed scalpel ready when Rick held out his hand for it. She watched him open an inch-long incision in the tough membrane, extending the puncture to open the surface of the brain beneath . . .

"There it is," Richardson said.

There was a small but intense clot with smeared edges and seeping blood behind it. The wound in the brain would heal itself, but the bleeder in there must be sealed. He would need a lighted retractor now. She held it ready.

He gave her an approving look.

"George, will you retract? Dr. Richardson you're going to need the suction tip next."

The lighted retractor inserted through the incision in the membrane gave Rick a clear picture. When he nodded Michelle knew what he was thinking. He would save this young woman who had come so close to death out there on the road. She was going to live. Michelle smiled as he gave a sigh of relief.

He straightened. "We'll approach it gently," he said. "Suction tip, Dr. Richardson."

The electric pump hummed softly as Richardson flipped the switch.

"Ready Doctor."

Rick, touched the hematoma lightly with the scalpel, and Richardson's hand moved into the bright light with the suction tip. He began to siphon off the dark blood from the disintegrating clot.

"Saline now. We'll irrigate it gently and clear it again."

Creighton leaned forward watching intently. "There it is!" he said abruptly.

A minute ruby had formed suddenly inside the tiny puncture in one of the convolutions of the brain.

Richardson looked at Rick, frowning. "That's it, all right, sir. But how can you get at it in there? You can't get the electrode in. And you can't ligate it without enlarging the incision. Without risking severing other tiny vessels that would be equally difficult to seal off."

Stone had straightened on his stool and was staring at Rick anxiously.

"Dr. Prentice," he said. "What are you going to do?"

"What would you do if it were your operation, Doctor?" Rick asked him.

"Surgery is your specialty," Stone said hastily. "Not mine. You rushed into this thing, not I. The decision and the responsibility are yours."

"We'll coagulate," Rick said. "A slight deviation from the kind of coagulation most of you are familiar with. But we'll coagulate the vessel just the same. Miss Lambert, I'll need a pair of fine-jawed forceps. No, something finer than that I think. Yes, those should do it."

He took them from her.

"Dr. Richardson, we have to seal off this vessel. Otherwise the condition and the hematoma will surely build up again, with a fatal termination. I'm going to touch the severed ends of the vessel with the tip of the forceps. And when I tell you to do so, you are going to touch the forceps with your electrode and coagulate through them. The gloves will insulate my hand. You'll need a steady hand. It is vital that your electrode should *not* touch any of the clamps, or the tissue of the brain other than through the forceps."

He left it at that, noting the expression in the resident's eyes. Richardson knew exactly what he meant. One slip and the patient would die.

"Clear the area for us again, George."

Michelle gave George Creighton the suction tip. He cleared the tiny wound again, and Rick bent with the forceps.

"Doctor . . . !" Michelle gasped.

The word had been wrung from her involuntarily. The patient's right arm had started to twitch as he touched the brain.

He spared her a reassuring glance. "We have to expect reflex movement. It's a reaction to the touch of the
58

forceps. But thanks, Miss Lambert. Carl, will you watch that?"

"Ready," Creighton said, stepping back.

"Ready with the electrode, Doctor?" Rick was bringing the forceps down steadily in rubber-gloved fingers, watching for the first minute ruby speck to appear. The tip of the forceps touched where the red speck formed. Rick held his breath, his fingers were rock steady.

"Now, Doctor," he said.

For an instant the electrode in Richardson's fingers hovered above the handles of the forceps, then it touched gently. The vessel hissed as the current touched it, turning the blood it contained into a blackened plug.

"You've done it!" Creighton said exultantly.

"Looks like it," Rick was saying. "We'll wait to make sure. Dr. Richardson is sweating, Miss Simon. A towel for him, please. We'll wait two minutes by the clock before we put in the plate and close."

It seemed a long two minutes to Michelle, but she supposed it was even longer to Rick as he studied the tiny wound and the blackened end of the vein.

"Dry and clean," his voice said at last, with satisfaction. "We'll begin the closure now."

The tension relaxed. The patient would live now, thanks to Dr. Rick Prentice. Michelle wondered if Bernice Randolf would ever really know how close she had been to death. She would be grateful to Rick if she did.

Passing curved needles with their trailing sutures, she began to wonder if the young woman on the operating table was really as attractive as everyone said.

chapter five

Dr. Prentice sat in the car outside the hospital. There was a long and difficult surgical schedule waiting for him inside, but this was not the reason why he was frowning thoughtfully. If he were to label the reason, he decided, he would call it expectancy.

When he walked into the operating suite he would see Michelle Lambert again. He was looking forward to that moment and he knew that Michelle was looking forward to his arrival too. After that the day would hold less frustration and they would both be happier.

He sighed as he acknowledged these feelings. He would ask her what plans she had for the weekend. He wanted to know if her friend Carla Simon was going to spend the weekend at Silver Sands and whether Michelle was going along. He was sure Bryan Meredith would also want to know.

He smiled as he remembered the weekend at Silver Sands. Then he remembered Michelle's brother lost in Vietnam. It was three weeks since he had written and he should have an answer to his letter soon. If anyone could discover her brother's fate, Colonel Anderson could. Anderson was attached to Intelligence over there, and finding the whereabouts and condition of men lost in enemy territory was his specialty.

He believed Lieutenant James Carson Lambert was

dead, but he hoped Anderson might prove him wrong.

If Lambert had gone down near the border zone he might have been observed by ground troops. Perhaps the boy was a prisoner now, held by the North Vietnamese.

But he did not want to think of that on such a sparkling morning. Michelle would ask him if he had heard yet, and he would have to say no. He had done what he could and now she must wait.

A pile of notes and reports waited on his desk. To save his time, they had been carefully sorted by his office nurse, Mrs. Barton.

She was talking on the phone as he came in. She put her hand over the mouthpiece and smiled at him, a plump blond woman with a pleasant face and merry eyes.

"Good morning, Doctor. I have Dr. Keller on the phone. He has a patient he'd like you to look at this afternoon, a Mrs. Terry. She has a goiter, and he'd like your opinion on surgery for it. He wanted you to see him this morning, but I told him your schedule here wouldn't permit it. Do you want to speak to him?"

He frowned. "Dr. Keller?"

"He has a practice like Dr. Stone's. A list of his patients would read like the Social Register. Some of Miss Randolf's friends have started talking about her operation, you can bet on it!"

He smiled at her obvious exultation. "That's good, Lisa?"

"Dr. Henry would have thought so, once he got used to the idea. It could take this place out of the red. A few patients like Mrs. Terry and the Randolf girl could subsidize the clinic. Will you speak to Dr. Keller?"

"You talk to him. I'll be seeing patients in my office at the usual time tonight. If Mrs. Terry is mobile he could send her around. If she's hospitalized tell him to call me here and we'll discuss it. I should be reasonably free from four to five this afternoon, unless something comes in through Casualty."

"Okay," she said. "But something had better not! I've

put Miss Randolf's report on top of the pile. She's been asking for you all morning. Miss Pringle has put a special in her room by request. Betty Falkiner from the presurgical women's ward."

"Thanks."

She went back to the phone. "Dr. Keller? I'm sorry to keep you waiting, Doctor. But I've contacted Dr. Prentice. He'd like to discuss Mrs. Terry with you this afternoon between four and five if that is convenient. It is? Good. Yes. Yes, Doctor. His office hours are from seven to nine tonight. He could see Mrs. Terry then, if you agree it's necessary. Thank you, Dr. Keller. Yes, I'm sure he would. Good-bye."

"You're sure he would what?" Rick asked, skimming over the top report.

"Be prepared to take some of Dr. Keller's surgical cases, Doctor," she smiled. "Dr. Keller seems to think it's what his patients are going to want now."

"Did he say that?"

"No. But that's what he meant."

He smiled. She was a loyal person, and genuinely pleased at what she obviously thought was an advantage to Hillside Hospital. She could be right.

The report on Bernice Randolf was in his hands. Frowning slightly, he said, "This is a good report, Lisa. Miss Randolf seems to be convalescing nicely. You said she was asking for me? There doesn't seem much need for that here."

"Maybe she wants to thank you. Is that so bad?"

"I'll see her. But Mrs. Ryan's case is more urgent, so we'll take Mrs. Ryan first."

"Mrs. Ryan is a clinic patient, Doctor," she reminded him, her eyebrows slightly raised as she studied him.

"Yes, I know. And since there are other patients also seriously ill in the clinic ward I couldn't very well see Mrs. Ryan without seeing them."

"No, Doctor. So shall I tell Miss Falkiner if she calls again that you'll see Miss Randolf at, say, eight forty?"

"What time am I due in the O.R.?"

"At nine, Doctor. The mitral stenosis is for ten o'clock."

"Then ten minutes with Miss Randolf should be enough this morning. I'd like to be up there before nine."

"Yes, Doctor. Is there anything else?"

He decided there wasn't, and he sorted quickly through the reports, choosing the ones on the clinic patients first. But there was something here he'd have to watch, something she had reminded him of in a roundabout way. If the clinic patients were as important as the Miss Randolfs who came here, so too were the Miss Randolfs as important as the clinic patients. It was as easy to lean too far one way as the other.

In the annex the nurses who would scrub in were already at work checking the equipment under sterilization. Michelle and Carla were talking quietly as they worked but became silent abruptly when Miss Pringle came in on her routine tour of the O.R. nursing staff. They continued their conversation automatically at the point where it had been interrupted when she had passed on to the next operating room.

"Well, there's one thing," Carla said as the door closed behind Miss Pringle. "The next time we swim out to Tern Isle in the moonlight, we'll check on the tide first."

"Carla, do you think I should go with you this time?" Michelle asked her friend. "I mean, it's your parents' beach house and I have never met them."

"They'd a lot sooner I went with you than alone, Michelle." She studied her friend obliquely. "But of course if you don't *want* to come with me? If you're not really interested in Rick?"

"It isn't that," Michelle said quickly. "It's just that I feel I'm imposing on you and your family."

"Nonsense! I like your company. I'm not sure I'll go if you won't come, and then Bryan will be disappointed. He mentioned it yesterday in the cafeteria. We managed to sit at the same table. It's three weeks since we were down there, and he thinks that's too long. He asked me if Rick had mentioned it."

"Rick may not be able to go."

"Did he say anything to you?"

Michelle frowned. "You know how busy he is."

"Then he'll mention it today, or tomorrow," Carla said with certainty. "And you'd better tell him you're going with me, or else!"

Michelle hesitated. "Well, okay," she said. "If he does ask me, I'll tell him you've invited me, and I'd like to go."

"That's better," Carla said with relief. "And you'll enjoy every minute of it. You know that. Anyway, they're working together in here on the heart surgery. Means they'll be scrubbing in together out there soon, with plenty of time to talk to one another."

"Simon! Lambert!"

They both jumped guiltily. Miss Pringle had returned unobserved and was studying them icily.

"Yes, Miss Pringle?" Carla ventured, red-faced.

"Miss Marsden and I expect our senior nurses in the operating suites to set their juniors a good example. I don't regard chattering when you should be concentrating on an instrument check as doing that. One of the tutor nurses is giving a lecture on operating room discipline in the lecture room on Saturday afternoon. I suggest you both attend it. Your memories, it appears, need some refreshing. Lambert, since you appear to have finished your check, I suggest you scrub immediately and begin setting out. Simon, if you're going to have your sutures ready when the surgeons come in, I suggest you stop talking and start working immediately."

"Yes, Miss Pringle," they muttered together.

She turned abruptly, and walked away from them.

Carla said in dismay, "Now see what you've done! We've lost Saturday afternoon for a stupid lecture we know by heart!"

"See what *I've* done?" Michelle said indignantly. "Well, I like that!"

64

But she hurried with her list to Kay Marsden, who took it from her, frowning.

"What was all that about?" Kay demanded anxiously.

"I was helping Carla on sutures. We were talking, and Miss Pringle caught us. We're to attend a lecture on O.R. discipline on Saturday afternoon."

"You should know better, both of you," Kay said sternly, but her brown eyes twinkled. "Okay. I'll try to get you off the hook when she cools down. But you'd better watch out! She'll check on you every now and then for a few days. And if she catches you gossiping again you'll really be in trouble."

"We'll see she doesn't, Kay,"

"Were you planning something? Like a weekend away?" Kay asked shrewdly.

"Yes we were."

"Well, I'll see what I can do. Now back to work."

"Thank you," Michelle said gratefully.

Down in the presurgical male ward Dr. Rick Prentice glanced at the clock on the wall. He did not want to check openly his wristwatch. It was eight forty and he should be in Miss Randolf's room now.

He smiled at his patient. "Is there anything else you'd like to ask me, Mr. Renner?"

"I guess not, Doctor."

"You still look worried. Is there still something you want to know about?"

"I guess it's just that I'm not used to hospitals, or doctors. Or being sick."

"You're lucky then. But you put up with quite a lot of pain before you went to see your doctor."

"Yes, I guess I did," the man mumbled.

"You'll have some pain again after your operation. But it won't be as bad as what you put up with before. And we'll make that pain easier for you by the use of sedation. I've explained the operation to you. It isn't a difficult one. It isn't even a dangerous one. It's something I've done before many times; you'd be surprised how many. I'm taking you in this morning at nine, and

65

you'll be back in your bed here soon after ten thirty. You'll walk better, stand better, and the danger of a clot of blood moving into your bloodstream from the congested vein in your thigh and stopping your heart will then have been eliminated. I want you to remember these things, and stop worrying. Okay?"

His patient managed to grin. "Okay, Doctor."

Rick patted his patient's shoulder and straightened. Not much time left to see Miss Randolf, but he'd have to make time. And it had been worthwhile, since he was leaving a calmer, a more confident patient behind him.

The private rooms were on the next floor, on the north side, with views toward Alcatraz Island.

The brown-haired nurse who opened the door to him had clear gray eyes and a pleasant smile.

"Good morning, Doctor."

"Good morning. Miss Falkiner, isn't it?"

"That's right, Dr. Prentice." She glanced at her patient and lowered her voice. "Miss Randolf has been asking for you all morning. She had a good night, but this morning she became restless. Dr. Creighton was in earlier. He ordered sodium bromide, and she's started to settle down again now."

She gave him the chart and he glanced at it, frowning. There was some slight increase in temperature, no doubt caused by her restlessness. Otherwise it was a very good chart.

"There doesn't seem to be very much the matter with her. Is she asleep?"

"Apparently, Doctor." The way she said it was a warning. She added, "Miss Randolf is an impatient young woman. When she wants something it has to be on hand at once."

He said aloud. "I'll try not to disturb her, if she's asleep. She needs rest."

He put the chart down and looked at the girl in the bed. And as though she sensed his presence, she moved restlessly, throwing one rounded arm out over the covers. The slim fingers were manicured. He wondered
66

if the lipstick and carefully applied makeup had been intended for his coming. She was certainly an attractive girl. Her face beneath the crown of spotless bandages was perfectly formed, with heavy, curling lashes over closed eyes, and full curving lips.

He remembered that she was a natural blonde with hair the color of cornsilk before it had been shaved for the operation. The expensive and revealing nightdress allowed a glimpse of her rounded breasts.

He became aware that he was thinking of her too much as a woman, and not enough as his patient.

She stirred again. Both arms came out from beneath the covers, and reached for him caressingly. He drew back startled. She caught one of his hands weakly in hers and then with sudden unexpected strength drew his hand down and pressed it against her, so that he felt the firm roundness of a breast through the filmy nightdress. He tried to release his hand, but her slender fingers held it fast, and now he could feel the fierce thumping of her heart.

She was awake. She had been awake all the time. That was what Miss Falkiner had meant by her veiled warning. His patient had been pretending, listening to what was said, waiting for him to come close.

Her eyes were open now, full of secret laughter as she held him fast. They were beautiful eyes, wide and almost violet in color.

"You've been neglecting me, Dr. Prentice! I've waited all morning and you wouldn't come." Her voice was husky, provocative, a slightly petulant voice.

The voice of a very spoiled young woman, one used to having her own way in all things, he decided angrily.

"I've been working here since eight, Miss Randolf." He freed his hand from her grasp gently. "You're doing so well there didn't appear to be any urgency. You have a very good nursing report. We're going to take the dressing off and examine you thoroughly later today when I have more time. There's a rather tight surgical schedule this morning. But I'm here now, so if there's something you want to ask me. . . ?"

He picked up her wrist, checking the radial pulse automatically.

"If my pulse is a little faster, that's your fault," she murmured, studying him from beneath her lashes. "It's because you're taking it."

He frowned. "You shouldn't say foolish things like that, Miss Randolf, and keep still please."

"Whatever you say, Doctor."

"Was there something you wanted to ask me?"

"There are quite a lot of things I want to ask you." She glanced at the hovering nurse. "But not while *she's* in here. Send her away."

He hesitated, with the nurse watching him.

"Do you mind, Miss Falkiner? Five minutes. I'm afraid I'm almost due in the operating suite."

"Five minutes?" his patient pouted at him as Betty Falkiner went out. "Rick, is that fair? When I've been waiting all morning to see you?"

He stared at her, hearing the door close behind Betty Falkiner. He said, "Who told you my name?"

"I know quite a lot about you, Rick. I've made it my business to find out. What's the matter? Don't you like me calling you Rick? I'm going to, whatever you say, so you might as well get used to it."

Closing the door, Betty Falkiner resisted an impulse to stand there quietly for a moment and listen. She would have given a lot to hear his reply.

Walking along the passage she wondered if Dr. Prentice would be calling his attractive patient Bernice when she returned. Maybe Dr. Prentice wasn't as confirmed a bachelor as everyone seemed to think. And who could remain distant where someone as attractive and wealthy as Bernice Randolf was concerned?

This was really something to make conversation interesting in the cafeteria at lunchtime. Not that it was Dr. Prentice's fault; Bernice Randolf was really giving him the treatment in there.

It must be hard for any man to resist a girl like that.

chapter six

Michelle's head ached slightly from the heat and the bright light in the operating room. Rick, assisted by George Creighton and Bryan Meredith, had repaired the mitral stenosis. They had cleared the orifice of the valve which had obstructed the free flow of blood from the auricle to the ventricle of the heart. The patient was breathing regularly.

George Creighton tied the last skin suture and the gaping hole in the patient's chest became a thin, pink line. Meredith sponged away the last smears of blood.

Rick asked wearily, "How's the pressure Carl?"

"Still 120 Doctor," Myers said from behind his screen. "All through?"

"Just about. We'll leave the cutdown tube in place for intravenous fluids or blood if its needed. But you can start taking out the endotracheal tube right away.

"That's it," he added. His smile was for Michelle first, before he looked around at the others. "Thanks, everyone. Carl, I'm coming through into the recovery room with you. I'll be down later, George."

"Good," Creighton said. He stepped down and began to pull off his gloves. "A satisfactory conclusion, I'd say. And just in time for lunch. Don't forget we have a varicotomy at two, Rick. What are you doing, Bryan?"

"Nothing more inspiring than an appendectomy,"

69

Meredith said, grinning behind his mask. "Anyway, it shouldn't take long. No complications expected."

He went out talking to Creighton. Rick pulled off his gloves. Carla was helping Myers take down his screen so that the patient could be removed to the recovery room. Michelle moved her trays and the few unused instruments, so that Kay Marsden could take away the now stained green sheets.

Rick Prentice was walking back toward her as Michelle wheeled out her instrument stand. His eyes smiled at her above his mask and he stood aside near the annex door, waiting.

"Tired?" he asked, sympathetically.

"Yes, I am. But not as tired as you, I guess."

"I recover quickly," he smiled. "I wanted to tell you that I haven't had a reply to my letter yet. I thought you'd want to know."

"Is that bad?"

"They say no news is better than bad news. It means my friend is still inquiring out there. He could still find something."

"I've been praying that he will."

"As soon as anything comes from him I'll let you know." He glanced past her, and noticed that they had begun to move the patient. He hesitated. "Bryan said that you might be going down to Silver Sands this weekend with Carla. Are you?"

"I've been thinking about it. Carla invited me. Why? Are you going again?"

"If I can possibly make it, I will. There's nothing I'd like better. And I think you and I should keep in touch until I do hear something. If that's all right with you. Is it?"

The way she felt about that was something she couldn't quite keep out of her expressive brown eyes. She nodded.

"If you want it that way, Rick."

"I do," he said. "I've never wanted anything more. I'd hoped to talk to you about that over lunch downstairs, if we could find a quiet place among the hungry.

70

But I should be in the recovery room now for some time —so that might not work out. Will you go to Silver Sands if I can't make it?"

She hesitated. "I'm not sure. Carla might not want to go alone. If Bryan is going I might tag along with Carla."

He looked his disappointment. "Of course."

"You had something else in mind?" she asked timidly.

"Well, I thought if we did happen to be both trapped here, we might get together for a late show and supper on Saturday night."

"Then shall we see what happens? I'd like that."

"You would? Good. I'll have to go now. I'll call you on Saturday if I don't have anything to report about your brother before that."

"I hope you do," she said. But as he walked away and she continued on with her tray she realized abruptly what that last sombre look he had given her meant. If he heard, he expected it to be bad news, not good.

If he thinks Jim's dead, she thought, it's because he knows more about what it's like over there. I have only intuition to go by. I can't believe that I'll never see my brother again. That's something that I feel, and nobody can convince me otherwise. Reason doesn't come into it. And perhaps knowing that, he agreed with me. He's good and kind. He's trying to find out about Jim for me.

"Did Rick say anything about the weekend just now?" Carla interrupted her thoughts. "I saw him talking to you . . . Hey there! You weren't fighting were you? What's the matter?"

She avoided Carla's searching eyes and forced herself to be calm. She had never spoken of her brother to Carla, or to anyone else at Hillside, except Rick. She had no wish to be discussed with pity. That could only make the waiting and the anxiety worse. She had confided in Rick for a different reason.

"Fighting? He asked me if I was going to Silver Sands, that's all."

"And you said yes, of course. Good! Hey there,

you're way behind. Look, I'll just fix these syringes and be right back."

"I thought you said you were having lunch with Bryan? You'd better not wait to help me. I won't be far behind you, and you might miss him. He has another operation at two. I heard him say so."

"At *two*?" Carla said in dismay. "All the same I thought it might work out as a foursome. Bryan and Rick lunch together when they can, you know."

"Rick can't. He expects to be in the recovery room for a while. And I don't intend to make your lunch with Bryan a threesome."

Carla shrugged. "Well okay. If you're sure you don't mind?"

"I don't mind."

She finished her work carefully and walked over to the canteen. Carla and Bryan were sitting alone together. She didn't want to disturb them and she was glad when she saw Betty Falkiner wave and smile at her. She waved back quickly in acknowledgment. She did not know Betty well, but she liked her. She was a cheerful, if talkative girl, one who smiled easily, and that was the kind of company she needed today.

Michelle put down her tray and sank gratefully into the chair. "That feels good! After four hours in the O.R. all I want to do is take the weight off my feet. It's worse than ward duty, and that's bad enough. Are you still in presurgical?"

"Not for the next week anyway. I'm specialing in one of the private rooms. Got a chair to sit in, and not much to do. Although my patient sees to it that I'm never idle for very long. She's like that. If she doesn't need something, she'll think of something for me to do. She has me up and down like a jack-in-the-box. Still, she's under sedation part of the time, and she has a locker full of the most gorgeous fashion magazines. So I'm not complaining. Aren't you going to ask me who it is?"

Michelle smiled. "Well, who is she?"

"I'm nursing Bernice Randolf!" Betty said triumphantly.

72

"Lucky you. What's she like?"

"Like I said. Spoiled is an understatement. Why is it that girls like her always get the things they want?"

Michelle sipped her coffee. "Because they have the money to buy them I suppose. It's partly habit too, and of course everyone says she is attractive."

"Do you think so?" Betty studied her skeptically. "Aside from the few million her father left her, what does she have that we haven't? Particularly you. You're just as attractive as she is. No, I think it's the other thing you mentioned. Habit. She's so used to having everyone come when she whistles, that she expects it. Therefore she gets it. It's psychological."

"Maybe. How is she?"

"How would you expect *her* to be? She's never looked back. A girl like Bernice Randolf always falls on her feet, even when she drives into a truck."

Michelle laughed. "I thought she fell on her head that time."

"You know what I mean, Michelle. When she wants something she gets it. And you'll see, that's the way it'll be with Rick Prentice."

Michelle swallowed. "With . . . Dr. Prentice, Betty? I don't understand you."

"She has a crush on Rick Prentice, that's what. And she doesn't care who knows it. Nobody could say she's bashful where men are concerned. So being Bernice Randolf and all that, she's going after him. And he wouldn't be male and human if he didn't respond, I guess, would he?"

"I don't know . . . !" Michelle said in confusion.

"Well, I *do*. That's because I've watched it happen from the start. She pumped me dry about him the first day. And she has everyone else who has been in her room since—the residents and nurses and even Dr. Stone when he comes to see her. Dr. Stone wanted to take her away from here the second day after the operation. He had an ambulance ready, but she wouldn't go. She told him she's going to spend her whole convalescence here under the care of the surgeon who saved her life. That's the way she put it to Dr. Stone. He argued but she wouldn't listen. She knew what she wanted—and that's what she'll get. It's like I told you."

"You mean she is in love with Dr. Prentice?" It hurt her to say it. There was a sick feeling starting deep within her. An unaccountable hurt.

"Maybe *she* thinks of it that way, as love," Betty said scornfully. "She's been throwing herself at him each time he comes in. I have to help her with her makeup when she knows he's coming. The nightgowns she wears! She was asking for him all this morning. Made me call his office at least a half dozen times. In the end I'd had it and I called Dr. Carter instead. She'd worked herself up into a temperature by then, so Carter gave her sedation. A sodium bromide tablet to settle down her restlessness. Dr. Carter gave her the tablet, and I held the glass. You know what happened? She slipped the tablet under her pillow when he wasn't looking. I found it later after Dr. Prentice had seen her and left for the operating room."

"You mean she only pretended to take it? But why?" Michelle was staring at her sickly. Strange impulses she couldn't control now prompting her to turn the knife in the wound, to hurt herself more deeply.

"Why? I'll tell you why. Because she knew as well as I did that she would have been asleep when Rick Prentice came in. I thought she *was* asleep. She pretended to be. When Rick came in I told him she was under sedation, and it was marked on the chart. But she was kidding. You know the first thing she did?"

"What?"

"He went to check her pulse, and she pretended to be half awake and tried to put her arms around him. He drew back, surprised, and looked at me. And she caught his hand put it here, and held it until he made her let go." She touched her own small breast with her hand, her gray eyes indignant as she remembered. "I pretended not to notice, of course. He was embarrassed. Then she opened her eyes and started telling him how hard she'd been trying to get him to come and see her. She accused him of neglecting her."

Michelle said slowly, in a low voice, "But surely Dr. Prentice could tell she hadn't had sedation. If he noticed her eyes. . ."

"Oh, he noticed her eyes all right," Betty Falkiner said vindictively. "How could he help noticing them, the way she was looking at him? But I doubt that he remembered right then that her pupils should have been enlarged. Anyway, if he didn't realize she'd cheated on the sedation, he will now. I put in my report about finding the tablet hidden beneath her pillow."

"Dr. Prentice wouldn't encourage her?" It was a difficult question to ask.

"No, I'll say that for him," Betty said triumphantly. "At least not then. He just asked her what it was she wanted to see him about. Were there questions she wanted to ask him about the operation. She said there were plenty, but she couldn't ask them while I was in there. How do you like that?"

"And he said?" It was as though she spoke about a stranger, about someone who did not interest her in the least. But that seemed to make it hurt more.

"I thought he was going to refuse. Maybe he couldn't think of a good excuse. Or maybe he just thought he owed it to her as his patient. He asked me would I mind leaving just for five minutes. He said he was due in O.R., and that was all the time he had. But I guess what he wanted was for me not to leave him alone in there for more than five minutes with Bernice. And you can be sure I didn't!"

"Five minutes isn't very long," she said.

"No? You'd be surprised how far a girl like Bernice could take a thing like that in five minutes. When I came back she was holding his hand and those blue eyes of hers were as wide as saucers. She was telling him that she was thinking of helping Hillside finance its clinic, she was so grateful for what he'd done for her."

"Surely Dr. Prentice couldn't fall in love with a girl like that?" she faltered.

"He doesn't have to fall in love. All he has to do is drift, and she'll do the rest. He wouldn't be the first man to marry some girl for advantages other than love. They're like that—the brutes. I'd say the clinic is as important to Rick as it was to his father. But you should know more about that than I do. After all, you work with him, I don't. What do you think?"

"I . . ." Michelle glanced across the big room at the clock, and stood up quickly. "Look at the time. I have to go."

"Michelle, you haven't touched your coffee, or your sandwich!"

"I'm not hungry today."

"I'm sorry I talked so much. I'd no idea you were in such a rush."

Michelle could stand no more, and rushed out of the canteen before Betty Falkiner could see the tears in her eyes. Frowning, Betty watched her go, and began to sense that something was wrong.

"Oh, no!" she thought in dismay. "I don't suppose Michelle could have a crush on Rick Prentice too?"

She looked around and saw Carla Simon. Carla would know. Carla was Michelle's roommate and in the same surgical team. She would have asked Carla right then, but she was sitting at a table with Dr. Meredith and they didn't look as though they would appreciate being interrupted.

Betty frowned uneasily. She liked to chatter, but she was no malicious gossip. She had never consciously hurt another girl that way, and she liked Michelle.

She began to think angrily and with growing dislike about the young woman in the private room, probably already thinking up new ways of capturing the handsome surgeon.

"I'd like to tell that dame exactly what I think of her!"

As he scrubbed, Rick Prentice found himself com-

76

paring Bernice Randolf with Michelle Lambert. He decided that they were opposites in more than just coloring, and the comparison did not favor his patient. Bernice was a spoiled and selfish girl. Maybe it was only the accident of birth that had made her so, but that was the way it was.

Yet in quiet moments he still saw those violet eyes of this morning, and knew that the warmth he had glimpsed in them was not all pretence. It was something he had noticed before. Something he had been noticing since she first opened her eyes in the recovery room after her operation, to discover him watching her there. And afterward, each time he went to see her he could not miss the sparkle in her eyes, or misconstrue it. If she hadn't already done so, Bernice Randolf was falling in love with him.

Changing from left hand to right, he thought about that soberly. It was not anything he had encouraged, or desired. But it was there. He had tried to brush the thought aside before. He tried now, but could not. It was, he was discovering, a thought that held both excitement and pleasure. Bernice was beautiful. She was also an extremely wealthy woman. He decided that her wealth was a very secondary consideration. If he were attracted to her, it was the woman who attracted him, not what she might do for the clinic.

He was going to make Hillside and the clinic self-supporting; he was going to do it without her help.

But there was the temptation. . .

This morning she had talked of a bequest in stock, the income from which he knew would put the clinic on a sound basis for years to come. It had seemed a vast gift to him, yet she had spoken of it as lightly as though it meant nothing to her.

He had told her that he had only done for her what any other surgeon might have done elsewhere. But she didn't see it that way. If she persisted in the bequest, he supposed there wasn't much he could do about it. He knew that the other board members would be delighted.

He might have felt that way himself, except for the

personal side. Except for the way she looked at him. The way she had pressed his hand against her breast.

He glanced at the clock. They would be waiting for him inside. Their silence as he came in through the door was broken by Myers' hearty voice beginning to tell a joke. They had been talking about him, he knew. And he was three minutes late by the wall clock.

He said, "I'm sorry, everyone. I was delayed with a patient." He met Michelle's dark eyes as he said it, and frowned as he saw that she was hurt. It prompted him to add in explanation, "This morning's patient was having a little trouble in the recovery room. Fortunately we were able to correct it. If everyone is ready we'll begin at once. Miss Simon, will you make a note of the time please. It's three minutes past two o'clock."

Handing him the knife for the first incision, Michelle avoided his eyes.

He had not needed to protest that he had been in the recovery room, and not in Bernice Randolf's private room. Nor had he needed to look at *her* the way he had when he said it. There was no bond between them, Michelle told herself, given and accepted. If they'd liked one another enough to kiss, so what? That didn't mean anything. Not really. They'd both kissed before. They'd both forgotten, and would again no doubt. There was no reason for her to feel hurt and bewildered, and suddenly so terribly, terribly lonely.

She fought back tears. Around her everything was as usual. George Creighton had started talking about golf as he worked, and Rick appeared to be listening since this was a routine operation, one which they had both performed so many times that their movements were automatic.

She was glad that her responses were automatic too, for today she was certainly not as alert as usual at all. She felt as she had the day she'd heard about Jim. That day she had kept it all—the pain, the hurt, and the loneliness—hidden deep inside her until the day ended and she reached the sanctuary of her room.

She remembered Dr. Henderson suddenly—bluff,

78

friendly Dr. Henderson. A great surgeon and a busy doctor, but a humane man who never failed to notice when one of his staff was in trouble. He had told her that she was wrong to do these things. Trouble was something that should be shared, not hidden, he had said. It hurt even worse when you kept it from your friends; it became intense. That way it could become a sickness deep within your mind.

He was right, of course. Her own training as a nurse had taught her that. But that was the way you were when you were shy. When you were so easily hurt, and felt pain so deeply, how could you change that?

It was something she had never learned to do.

"The other retractor, Michelle. The small one please."

"I'm sorry, Doctor!"

She corrected her mistake quickly, aware of George Creighton's slightly puzzled glance. He was not used to her making mistakes.

"Are you okay, Michelle?" he asked, studying her.

"Yes, Doctor."

She must be more careful, she decided. She tried to be, but she wasn't. She kept remembering the things that Betty Falkiner had said. She dropped a hemostat, and made the beginner's mistake of moving instinctively as though to pick it up before she could control the impulse. Things went from bad to worse. She fumbled her passing, red-faced and confused.

The operation became a nightmare to her. Both surgeons avoided looking at her. She was grateful for that, aware that she deserved less. Kay Marsden had noticed and was watching her anxiously; so was Carla.

She allowed herself a sigh of relief when it was over, and the surgeons stepped back, pulling off their gloves. She trundled her instrument stand out, avoiding looking at anyone, and automatically began cleansing and sterilizing her instruments.

Carla came in and left her suture trays to come over to her. "For heaven's sake, Michelle, what was the matter in there? You sick, or something?" she asked anxiously.

"No, I'm okay."

"Then what happened? Rick say something to upset you?"

"No, of course not. He hardly said anything, and I deserved to be bawled out. It was just one of those days, I guess. Haven't you ever made mistakes?"

"Who me? Plenty! Everyone does. But it's the first time I've seen you do it. So it has to have a cause—like what made it one of those days for you anyway?"

"How do I know? Maybe I made so many mistakes I became confused."

"You're sure it isn't Rick?"

She managed to look at her friend calmly. "Really, Carla! I can't account for it. It was just one of those things. So can't we just forget it?"

Carla shrugged, frowning as she studied her. "Okay! If that's the way you want it. Maybe you're just tired. It gets us all. You really need another weekend up at Silver Sands, don't you? Maybe we can leave earlier this time. I had lunch with Bryan, and he says he's going to try to do that. We can surf together tomorrow afternoon then, the four of us, if Rick can get away."

"Carla, would you take over inside for a moment. I'd like to speak to Michelle."

They both looked up quickly as Kay Marsden walked briskly toward them. Carla gave Michelle a sympathetic glance.

"Sure, Miss Marsden. Right away."

Michelle straightened and looked at the supervisor. "I'm sorry, Miss Marsden. I can't account for being so clumsy in there. It just seemed to happen. And when I began to worry about it, it just got worse."

"It usually does. You're not ill?"

"No, not really. I have a headache but I think what happened in there gave it to me."

"Well, you're being frank at least. Mary Glassop is on stand-in. The headache could mean any number of things. I'm relieving you of duty for the rest of the day,

80

Michelle. Report to Mrs. Patterson and she'll give you some aspirin. Glassop will finish your shift. You've been working too hard. If you don't feel better Mrs. Patterson will send for one of the doctors."

"I'm sure I'll be quite all right in the morning, Kay," She saw a way out suddenly. "Why not let me work tomorrow? I wouldn't mind working all day, or being on stand-in in the afternoon, and I'm sure I'd be okay."

Kay studied her, frowning slightly, puzzled. Her nurses always grasped any chance that occurred where leave was concerned.

She said shrewdly, studying Michelle, "I thought I heard you and Carla talking about going to the Simon's beach house for the weekend?"

"Carla did invite me, but . . ."

"Might be exactly what you need," Kay Marsden interrupted. "Better give it consideration before you decide to work instead. I can't think of anything more relaxing than a weekend at a quiet beach. Carry on now. I'll get your relief in here as quickly as I can. And you can forget about working tomorrow. I can't *make* you spend a relaxing weekend with Carla. I can only tell you that it's what *I* think you should do. But it will probably be that or a weekend in the infirmary when the house mother hears you're off duty with a headache. Mrs. Patterson hasn't had a patient in her infirmary to fuss over for a long time. She complains all the time about our girls being so disgustingly healthy. I've laid it on the line for you, Lambert. It's up to you which it is to be—Patterson's pills, or Silver Sands. I know what *I'd* choose!"

chapter seven

Rick Prentice drank the last of his coffee and stubbed out his cigarette. George Creighton was getting up reluctantly from the depths of one of the lounge chairs in the surgeons' rest room.

George was tired, and he looked it.

"Have you seen Miss Randolf today, Rick?" he asked.

"This morning on rounds. I'll look in before I leave the hospital again. Why, George?"

"Did she tell you I was in to see her this morning?"

"Yes, she mentioned it. She said she discussed the clinic with you."

"That's so. Asked so many questions she made me dizzy. There's a shrewd mind behind that lovely face, Rick."

"I never doubted that George," Rick smiled. "She is also a very spoiled young woman, who expects her own way in everything. As a matter of fact I told her she can go home tomorrow."

Creighton said slowly, "I wouldn't lose touch though, Rick. Bernice seems genuinely interested in the clinic. She said, I quote: 'I owe Hillside a great deal, Dr. Creighton. Perhaps my life.' Just like that. Then came all the questions about the clinic, what it meant to *you*, and what it cost to maintain. I had the feeling that it was you she was grateful to, not Hillside."

Rick shrugged. "You know how they are, George. While they're ill, they're grateful; they want to do something for us in return. When they recover they have second thoughts. Nothing ever comes of it. We've both seen that happen."

"That's so. But it can be different when there's some personal interest or involvement, Rick. It seemed to me that Bernice Randolf is more interested in the surgeon than the clinic. That being so, it could be different. And the kind of fund *she* would establish might lift us out of the red."

"You're joking about the personal interest, George."

"No, I'm serious. She's an attractive woman, Rick," George Creighton said soberly.

"Attractive? Yes, she is. But so are other girls."

"Except that you don't seem to notice them. And none of our acquaintances has her wealth, or her power. It was just a thought. Anyway, don't kill any impulse she might have to help the clinic along."

Rick frowned. "If she really wanted to help the clinic I'd be the last one to stop her. But I doubt that she will."

Creighton studied him for a moment. "You said that with so much certainty I wonder if you're expecting some condition you might not like."

Rick laughed. "Hardly. As for the clinic, we're starting the construction work on the obstetrical ward on Monday. Arthur Dickinson expects to move in within a month. After that a lot of our worry about the clinic is going to be over, whether some benefactor establishes a fund or not. Arthur is delighted with the plans we've made, and he's convinced it's going to be a success."

Creighton smiled wearily. "That's true, and I agree with Arthur and you on that. All the same, if the lovely Bernice wants to help, don't let her get away. The board would skin you, if you did. Even with Arthur Dickinson's patients, we could still use that kind of help."

Rick walked out slowly with him, leaving him at the elevators. He chose to use the stairs instead of waiting, and climbed briskly to the private wing. Maybe it was just as well he had told Bernice Randolf she could go home in the morning, he decided. He found her attractive, though not in the same way Michelle Lambert attracted him. He had noticed himself turning automatically toward Bernice's room on the rare occasions when he had a little time on his hands. Not that there was any harm in that. It had just become a rather insidious habit, he told himself as he left the stairhead and turned toward her door.

She had learned to recognize his step outside her door, and he invariably found her waiting eagerly as he came in. Today would be no exception, he knew, even though she had become annoyed about going home when he mentioned it this morning.

It might have been wiser to have visited this room less frequently, but it was too late now for such a decision.

Hospitals were small places and nurses gossiped easily. As he tapped on the door and heard the brisk steps of the nurse approach, he wondered if Miss Falkiner had drawn any mistaken conclusions from his frequent visits to her patient; he hoped not.

"Yes?" Betty Falkiner's expression was angry but as she recognized him she adjusted the professional mask quickly. "Good afternoon, Dr. Prentice. I wasn't expecting you back so soon." She stood aside. "I was just leaving. Do you need me here before I go?"

"Go where?" he asked, frowning, turning his head to look at his patient. She was watching from a chair near the window.

"Miss Randolf has decided she no longer needs a nurse in here," Betty Falkiner said, glancing back at her. "Miss Pringle said I could finish the shift back in my own ward. But if you need me before I leave?"

He looked past her at Bernice Randolf, and his patient said in her clear, arrogant young voice: "I don't need a nurse in here any more, Rick. Why should I when I'm leaving in the morning? There must be a lot of other patients who need her more than I do. I told Miss Pringle that, and she agreed."

There was something here that he could not understand, a strong hostility, barely concealed by their calm voices and innocuous words.

"Miss Pringle has been here?" he asked mildly.

"No, I called her."

"In that case, you may go, Miss Falkiner. No doubt Miss Pringle knows where you're needed most."

Betty Falkiner's lips firmed noticeably. "Yes, Doctor."

"I'd like to thank you before you leave though, for nursing my patient so well." He looked at Bernice. "You were lucky to have Miss Falkiner here. You were still seriously ill when you were brought in here. Miss Falkiner is one of our senior nurses and most efficient. As your surgeon I was both surprised and pleased when Miss Pringle chose her to nurse you."

"Oh? I thought this was *your* hospital, Rick. Not Miss Pringle's," Bernice murmured sarcastically.

He smiled. "Then you don't know a great deal about hospitals, Miss Randolf. The Director of Nursing Services makes the decisions where the nursing staff is concerned."

"I'm not ungrateful, Rick," Bernice Randolf said stiffly.

"May I go now Doctor?" Betty Falkiner asked icily. "They're short-staffed in the ward."

"Yes, of course, Betty." He opened the door for her and gave her a reassuring smile that she answered with an eloquent glance toward his patient as she went out.

He closed the door gently behind her.

"I wasn't just making conversation when I said Miss Falkiner is a good nurse. She is one of our best."

Bernice was pouting at him from beneath her turban of bandage as he walked toward her. She said petulantly, "She was insolent to me, Rick! I detest insolence in anyone like that."

He frowned, looking down at her. "You said that as

85

though she was a maid in your apartment. She isn't, you know. She's a highly skilled professional nurse, and was responsible for your care in here."

"You're taking her side against me," she muttered.

"No. I'm just trying to find out what has disturbed my patient, and antagonized her nurse."

She got up quickly and turned her back upon him and walked to the window to stare out. He resisted an impulse to follow her there. She walked firmly, he noticed. She had recovered well. She had not even lost much weight. Through the thin nightdress and robe her youthful, lovely figure was etched against the light outside.

He looked away uneasily.

"If you must know, Rick," she said bitterly over her shoulder, "she kept refusing to send for you when I asked her to."

"You were ill?"

"I wanted to talk to you. Alone." She turned to face him angrily. "Is that too much for a patient to ask, to see her doctor alone?"

He smiled, relieved. So that was all it was.

"Miss Falkiner would know when I was operating, or with other patients. I've probably seen you more often than I have any other patient recently, Bernice," he said. "But it isn't possible to come when you call. Unless in emergency. She would know that."

"Do I have to be *dying* to see you alone?" she demanded fiercely.

"No, of course not. But you must be reasonable about such things . . ."

"I don't feel reasonable today! Anyway I knew you'd come in this afternoon, so I called Pringle and had her move Falkiner out of here. That way I knew I'd be able to talk to you alone."

She walked toward him. There were tears in the blue-violet eyes, and her full lips were trembling.

"It isn't good for a girl to think too much about her doctor when she has been injured as you were, Bernice," he said uneasily.

86

"Why? Because she might become attracted to him? You're a little late with your advice, Doctor. I know what I feel for you."

"Bernice, many women have thought themselves in love with their physician and discovered later that they'd mistaken gratitude for love."

"I love you, Rick. And why not? You're not married. You're not engaged to another girl. There's no other girl in your life; and you are interested in me. Don't deny it. I've seen it in your eyes when you look at me. It's there now."

"You're a very lovely woman, Bernice," he said gently. "You'd rouse the interest of any man. But you must listen to me."

"No, you listen to me, Rick," she said in a low voice. "Does the clinic mean so much to you? Together we could make it greater than your father ever dreamed it could be. Isn't that what you want? Isn't it Rick?"

His smile was wry, and held no mirth. "If I fall in love, Bernice, it will be with the woman, not with what the wealth might do for the clinic."

"But if the two went together, what then? If you loved her, would you refuse her help? How *do* you really feel about me, Rick? When we're close like this can you say you don't want me? Can you say truthfully that you couldn't love me?"

She was holding his shoulders now, forcing him to look deeply into her eyes.

"Do you understand what I'm saying, Rick?"

"Yes, I understand."

"Then you must realize that I love you, Rick," she was whispering. "I love you! Only you. Could you hurt me, or refuse me, knowing that? Rick, how do you feel about me?"

Her lips were coming up to claim his, and he felt the warmth of her body pressing to him eagerly through the flimsy robe.

Through the surge of fierce response as her lips pressed his in a lingering kiss, he heard the door open.

"Betty, can you spare a moment?" a masculine voice

asked pleasantly. It broke off. *"Excuse me!"* it said, startled.

The door began to close again.

Rick was holding her away from him. He turned, still holding her, recognizing Barry Moreton. He forced his voice to calm.

"Dr. Moreton, come in here, please."

Moreton looked past him at Bernice, and hesitated. "Yes Doctor," he said uncertainly. He came inside and closed the door.

"Miss Randolf is a little upset," Rick said calmly. "Miss Falkiner has been recalled to ward duty. Will you stay with her until I send a nurse in? She needs mild sedation. Under the circumstances I'll leave that to you." He avoided her eyes, which were becoming accusing now, and beginning to show hurt and dismay.

"Yes, of course, Doctor," Moreton said. "Miss Randolf, let me help you." He was taking her from Rick gently. Not sure now exactly what he *had* seen from the doorway.

Rick looked back at her. The hurt was gone; it was replaced by anger.

"You must rest tonight, Miss Randolf," Rick said quietly. "I'll see you in the morning. With rest, you should be ready to go home by then."

She said nothing as he closed the door behind him.

Through the windows of the infirmary in the Nurses' Home, Michelle had watched the lights come on in the hospital.

At Mrs. Patterson's insistence, Dr. Harker, Hillside's senior medical service resident, had examined her earlier in the afternoon. He had prescribed mild sedation, which at the moment made her feel calm and rather vague. He had suggested, when Mrs. Patterson was out of hearing, that if she had friends she could spend the weekend with, she should get away from the hospital. That might be better for her than anything he or the house mother could do to help her.

It seemed strange when she thought about it, how

88

everyone was prompting her to return to Silver Sands this weekend. A week ago she would have needed no prompting. But now, what was there for her at Silver Sands?

She sat up slowly in the chair, puzzled as she studied her surroundings in the moment before memory returned and the vagueness of sleep and sedation faded. A nurse dozed in a chair beside her. It must be late, very late.

Michelle sat up abruptly. "For heaven's sake, Carla!" she said. "You'll give yourself a stiff neck, going to sleep that way! Carla, wake up."

"Eh? What. . . ?" Carla stared at her briefly, her blue eyes surprised. "Did I go to sleep?"

"Did you? And you're the one who said *I* could sleep hung on a clothes line!" Michelle smiled. "Really, Carla! If Mrs. Patterson came in and saw you like that she'd have you undressed and in the next bed before you could escape!"

"Which might not be such a bad thing, the way I feel right now," Carla admitted, yawning. "Been a hard day. We missed you in there, believe it or not. How are you? Bruce Harker said it was nothing desperate. More emotional fatigue than anything was the way he put it."

"There's nothing the matter with me," Michelle protested. "I'll be just fine tomorrow." She broke off. "Is that what Bruce Harker said?"

"You'll be just fine on Monday morning, when we get back from Silver Sands. And Bruce did say that, when I asked him about you. He's not far wrong, is he Michelle?"

Michelle avoided her candid blue eyes in sudden confusion. "I'm sure I don't know what would make anyone think that."

"No? All your friends are worried about you; that's what two of us think, at least. Bryan and I. And maybe others. They've all been in to see you tonight, but you were asleep so we decided not to disturb you. Kay and all the girls from O.R. And Bryan of course. I sent the girl in here off to get herself some coffee. I thought you'd wake, and the chair looked comfortable."

"It was very good of you, Carla."

"Nonsense. I wanted to. Besides, I had another reason. Rick came in twice. When he came in the second time I told him I'd stay. I said I'd call him when you woke."

"Carla, please don't!" she said in dismay.

"A promise is a promise." She glanced at the clock. "He won't come back to visit again tonight. It's too late. He's gone home. But the least you can do is talk to Rick on the phone. He's worried about you, and he agrees with Bryan and me that the best possible therapy for you is a weekend at Silver Sands with us. Even if he can't make it. And that's exactly what you're going to do even if Bryan and I have to kidnap you to get you there!"

"I couldn't go back there now." She hadn't meant to say it that way, but that was the way it came out.

"Why not?" Carla had her hand on the phone. "Because of Rick?"

"It isn't anything I want to talk about, Carla," she said.

Carla studied her. "It can't be anything Rick did at Silver Sands," she said. "That's for sure. Since about all he did there was save your life, be sweet to you all the time, and maybe kiss you once or twice. So it's something that happened here. Since our weekend together."

"I told you I just don't want to talk about it." Michelle murmured. "And it isn't anything Rick's done. How could it be? I don't have any claim on him. He's perfectly free to do whatever he pleases. . ."

"So that *is* it," Carla said thoughtfully. "Bryan and I are right. Bruce Harker too, though we have more inside information than Bruce has. I know exactly what's the matter now."

"You do?"

"I do! You've been listening to those stupid rumors about Rick and the Randolf girl that Betty Falkiner started. Wait! Wait! You got it from Betty herself, didn't you? The day you had lunch with her, and I was with Bryan?"

"I. . ."

"So that's it! Because you're in love with Rick it hurts. So when you had to work with him yesterday. . ." She broke off abruptly and moved to sit beside her friend and put her arms around her. "Hey there, no tears! Stop it at once."

But the tears were already flowing. "I . . . can't help it! Or the way I feel . . . !" Michelle sobbed.

"Now you listen to me, Michelle," her friend said, hugging her. "If you'd seen him in here tonight, you'd know it was *you* he was worrying about, not that spoiled socialite. If he isn't already in love with you, he's on the way. Honest, I mean that. Even Bryan's noticed."

"Now you see why I can't go to Silver Sands again. . ."

"No, I don't see. If Rick can't make it, there'll be just the three of us there. There won't be any problem for you. You can surf and laze around, and just do whatever you feel like doing. You'll be a lot better able to face things on Monday, including Rick. You'll see."

"I'd spoil your weekend," she protested glumly.

"No you won't. We both like having you around."

"If Rick goes, I just couldn't."

She was weakening, Carla decided, and that seemed a good sign. She said quickly, "And why not? What do you really want, anyway, Michelle? If a girl wants a guy and there's any doubt about him feeling the same way, she has to go after him. You can't walk away and leave him like a ripe peach for someone else to pick. Not with a girl like Bernice Randolf around with itchy little fingers. If you think Bernice would leave him like that for you, darling, you're crazy! She's going after Rick with everything she has. That's what made Betty so mad at her. Mad enough to start those rumors."

"Betty didn't know she was hurting me."

"Did she hurt you? Did she tell you Rick was making

91

passes at Bernice? Of course she didn't. It was the other way around. That was what made Betty so mad—but not at Rick. Rick's interested in *you*, Michelle. He was interested in you that weekend, before he knew Bernice, or had seen her. You have an advantage there, and if you're sensible you'll keep it. I'm going to call Rick right now. . ."

"Carla, no! I just couldn't talk to him tonight. Not after what we've been saying."

". . . and you're going to calm yourself and take the call," Carla said as though she'd noticed no interruption at all. She flicked the single digit that called the switchboard. "Miss Simon calling from twenty-nine. Get me Dr. Prentice, please. Yes, I know he left the hospital hours ago. Call him at his apartment. He's waiting for this call."

Michelle waited, listening with Carla, trying to answer her sympathetic smile. She was aware that she was trembling and that tears were still close.

"Hello, Rick," Carla said. "Yes, she's awake. Much better, I'd say. She's agreed to come to Silver Sands with us tomorrow and that might be exactly what she needs. But she'll want to tell you about that herself. Here she is."

The phone was in her hand. She looked at it uncertainly, hearing Rick's concerned voice.

"Michelle? Are you there, Michelle?"

"Yes, Rick." It didn't sound like her voice, but it was clear, and it sounded calm.

"You had me worried tonight! How do you feel now?"

"A little foggy from sedation, but otherwise okay. I'm sorry I was asleep when you called. Dr. Harker doesn't seem to think there's much wrong."

He hesitated before he said bluntly, "Harker doesn't have the personal interest in you that I have, Michelle. It wasn't the concern of a doctor for a patient that I felt. But if you're feeling better now, that's fine. Carla said you're going to Silver Sands with her. That should

92

relax you again. But no more swimming out to Tern Isle at the top of a big tide. Promise?"

"I'm hardly likely to do that," she said in a low voice. "Not again."

"And yet, I'm glad that you did that once. We might never have learned to know one another as we do do now, if you hadn't." Rick said softly. "Harker said that your trouble seemed emotional. That makes me feel guilty."

"Oh? Why should you, Rick?"

"Because I haven't had any news of your brother. It was that, wasn't it? I've written to my friend over there, now all I can do is ask you to wait a little longer. I have a confession to make there, Michelle. When you told me about it, when you confided in me, I have to admit that I felt certain Jim had been killed. But I've changed that belief."

Her heart leaped. "Rick, have you heard something?"

"Oh, no!" he said quickly. "Don't misunderstand me! But you've never wavered in your belief that he's alive someplace. Never once. Somehow I've come to believe that a faith like that must be rewarded. With each day that passes without a reply to my letter, my belief in that strengthens. I can't say more than that now. Like yours, I'm afraid mine isn't a belief based on reason either. But it's there, and it persists."

She couldn't find words to reply.

He said presently, "Michelle? Are you still there?"

"Yes," she said.

"There's just one other thing I wanted to say. Carla has probably told you that I'm undecided about going to Silver Sands this weekend. It could be difficult for me to leave town. I suppose I've rather taken it for granted that you . . . liked my company the last time, and that you wanted me to come if possible. But now, I'm not so sure about that. I feel the need to be sure. Maybe it was presumptuous of me? Michelle, do you really want me to be there?"

She sensed the approaching hurt again. Slowly she

said, "Isn't that up to you, Rick? You have a beach house there. I mean, if you want to come . . ."

"Then it isn't really important to you that I be there?"

Did she sense hurt in his voice? She could not be sure. "If there's something more important that you want to do, I'll understand, Rick," she said.

"You must go just the same though, even if I can't make it. You need this weekend. Promise?"

"I've already promised Carla."

"Well, at least I can be glad of that," he said with a kind of forced cheerfulness. "You'll feel better on Monday. Maybe we both will. Think of me when you're surfing with the others. I'll certainly be thinking of you. I would have let the other thing go if you really needed me at Silver Sands. But it is important to me too in a different way. I may as well tell you that someone wants to establish a fund to finance the clinic. George Creighton called me tonight to say an attorney had contacted him about it, and it seems that some private discussion with the principal is necessary this weekend."

"I see," she said, trying to keep the bitterness from her voice. "I hope your negotiations are successful, Rick. I know how much that means to you. Good night."

"Michelle, wait. . ." His voice had changed abruptly, become uncertain. She did not answer. She put the phone down slowly and looked at Carla.

Carla had retreated to a discreet distance but she was scowling at her fiercely.

"If there's something more important that you want to do, I'll understand," she mimicked. "Michelle! What on earth are you doing to yourself? If that wasn't a brush-off, I've never heard one! Honestly! I just don't understand you!"

She said quietly, "I'm not Bernice, Carla. I just found that out. I'm me. You were right. I love Rick. But he doesn't feel the same way about me."

Carla's arms were around her again and Carla was murmuring words of comfort, mixed with anger against Rick Prentice and the world of men.

94

chapter eight

Michelle and Carla stared together at the familiar silver crescent of sand with the smooth surf breaking upon it.

"Well, at least Silver Sands is still the same," Carla said grumpily, "And the weather's fine. As for the men in our lives, who needs them anyway?"

Michelle smiled. Carla did for one, she knew. As for herself, she was not sure any more. Carla had been moody and irritable ever since Bryan Meredith called before they left the hospital telling Carla that he couldn't come with them as they had planned this afternoon.

"Do you think Bryan will make it tonight?" she asked Carla.

"He said he'd try," Carla replied gloomily. "But it could be late when he gets here. He said if it was, he'd see us for an early morning swim. Why do they have to hold an emergency board meeting on a Saturday night?"

"It isn't Bryan's fault," Michelle said soothingly. She had been wondering about the board meeting throughout the drive. Wondering if there was a connection with Rick Prentice's discussions with Bernice Randolf. She said hesitantly, "Do you suppose it concerns the clinic fund?"

"I've been wondering about that." Carla frowned at the sea. She glanced sidelong at Michelle, remembering that her friend had troubles too. "Bryan did say that George Creighton called him, and George was driving him to the meeting someplace downtown. If they are meeting Bernice Randolf, at least Bryan and George will be with Rick. I mean, it's not just a private something between Rick and Bernice."

Michelle did not want to think about it. She said quickly, "Bryan will be here in the morning, you'll see. Carla, let's settle in and change for the surf right away, shall we?"

Carla nodded. "No sense in wasting sunshine. Am I glad you came along! It would have been pretty grim here alone today. We'll have a cocktail to cheer us both up, and surf all afternoon. Okay?"

"Okay!" Michelle agreed, smiling.

And she wouldn't think about Rick all afternoon, Michelle told herself firmly.

Only it wasn't as simple as that, she knew. When you felt the way she did about Rick, it wasn't something you could turn on and off at will. Everything she saw here must remind her of him. But today Carla needed her companionship, and she was going to give her that. Carla was disappointed and miserable, perhaps helping Carla would make it easier for both of them.

So she was bright and cheerful at the cottage. She found she could look at Tern Isle and the sea beyond and remember only good moments there. The good moments had been many, and for a little while she told herself firmly she had had something with Rick that had been hers alone. Neither Bernice Randolf or anyone else could take that away from her now.

They changed quickly and Carla made strong cocktails. They began to laugh and chatter again as the drinks and the sun warmed their bodies and relaxed them.

They surfed until they were tired and then lay in the sun on the warm sand. Several times Michelle discovered Carla studying her curiously and she knew

96

exactly what Carla was thinking; that she had recovered quickly, that perhaps her feeling for Rick had not been love at all. . .

It would be different tonight though, Michelle knew. As the afternoon waned she began to dread the night.

The worst time came when the day ended, supper was over and the dishes put away. They sat in the lounge with the drapes drawn back from the windows and music drifting from the stereo. At another time they would have both felt pleasantly tired and relaxed. Carla had made two highballs for a nightcap.

Through the open windows Michelle could hear the surf pounding sullenly on the other side of Tern Isle. There was a moon again. Not a full moon this time, but a golden crescent of new moon above the palms painting the same silver track across the channel toward them.

Ice clinked in Carla's glass as she put it down. She stood up and turned off the stereo.

"For heaven's sake," she said. "Let's just go to bed. We're sitting here like two zombies. For a while there this afternoon I began to think you were over it. But you're not; that was just for my benefit, wasn't it? And here I've been feeling sorry for myself all afternoon, when I know darned well Bryan will be here in the morning."

Michelle smiled. "You're in love with Bryan, aren't you, Carla?"

"It isn't indigestion making me feel this way. So, yes, I suppose I am. He's one of those characters who grow on you."

"He's a great guy, Carla. You'll be happy with Bryan."

"Maybe. Michelle, are you sure that you and Rick are through?"

"Carla, do you mind? I don't want to talk about that, not here, not tonight."

"That's understandable, I guess. But there's one thing I must say; something Bryan told me. He assisted Rick this morning. They brought in a guy to Emergency last night from a road accident. Bryan said he'd never seen Rick as irritable and depressed as he seemed this morning. Nothing went right in there, and at one time Bryan thought they were going to lose the patient. He doesn't know what happened between you, but he asked me if you two had been quarreling."

"What did you tell Bryan?"

Carla frowned. "Well, I was still boiling about last night. So . . ." She hesitated.

"Carla, what *did* you tell Bryan?"

"Well, I said if Rick was feeling depressed and irritable this morning I was glad. I hoped he keep right on feeling that way, only more so. I said that it wasn't anything you'd done that was causing it; and that any guy who fell for Bernice Randolf deserved what he got."

"Carla, you didn't!" Michelle cried, appalled.

"Didn't I though! And I might have told him a lot more too, except that he started laughing at me as though it was some kind of joke. He said he'd never seen Rick as interested in any girl as he was in you. If you two broke up he said he knew darned well it wouldn't be anything Rick wanted. I blew my top with him about then and hung up. But later, driving down, I kept thinking about what he'd said. Bryan believes what he said, Michelle, I'm sure of that. And he knows Rick better than anyone else does at Hillside."

Michelle stared at her numbly. "Carla, are you blaming me?"

"No," she said gently. "Not blaming you. Not at all. But I *am* wondering if you might be wrong about the way Rick feels. And if that's so, if this is all a misunderstanding, Rick might be feeling as hurt and miserable as you are tonight. Now, let's sleep and forget it, shall we? Bryan will be here in the morning and maybe we'll all feel better. I'm going to give you two of Bruce Harker's tablets and borrow one for myself."

Sleep did not come easily to Michelle, even with the tablets. Carla had been breathing deeply and evenly in the other bed for a long time, but Michelle was still staring at the moonlight and listening to the distant surf. She kept going over and over in her mind the things that had happened between Rick and herself. She decided Carla was right about some things. Betty Falkiner had never said Rick was making passes at Bernice. Or that he had responded to Bernice. His response was just something that *Betty* considered inevitable, and she had gone along with Betty on that.

She too had thought Bernice's beauty and wealth must be irresistible. Was it to Rick? Might not Bryan know the answer to that better than anyone else?

Was it her own shyness, her feelings of inadequacy that had made her so sure that Rick would turn to Bernice Randolf at the first opportunity?

Rick had asked her did she want him at Silver Sands. She had never wanted anything so much in her life, but she had told him if he had something more important to do, to go do it. Could she be sure now that she hadn't driven him further from her and closer to Bernice?

But that wasn't the way it was at all, she thought desperately. I thought if he loved Bernice, if he really wanted her, I'd just . . . step down! When you love someone you *want* them to be happy.

Perhaps, she decided, that was where her fault lay. If she had given Rick the answer he wanted, he might have been here tonight. . .

Michelle wakened reluctantly from a deep sleep. Somewhere, someone was knocking. It was an impatient pounding.

She heard the door open and Carla's sleepy voice said, "Hello Bryan. What's the emergency?"

"I've been knocking for ten minutes. It's past sunup. Must be seven at least."

"Seven! We both just turned over for the second time, and if you think . . ."

Bryan interrupted, "I drive half the night to get here so that I can keep our early morning date, and you haven't even said hello. Come here!" A scuffle started and Carla giggled.

"Hello," Carla said in a changed voice.

It grew very still out there. Michelle smiled sleepily and yawned. She changed into bikini, beach coat and sandals and was brushing her hair when Carla came in.

"Michelle! Bryan's here. He. . ." Carla broke off. "Heavens! You're way ahead of me!"

"I'll make us all some coffee while you're getting ready. Did Bryan drive here this morning?"

Carla decided there was a different question in her eyes. "He drove here last night, after the meeting, so he could keep our date this morning. Rick stayed in town."

"I'll make the coffee now."

Carla put a hand on her arm. "Michelle, wait," she said in a lower voice. "Rick had to go back to his apartment on some business of his own. Bryan didn't know what it concerned. But he sent you a message. He's coming here later today and he wants to see you."

She stood very still suddenly. "Rick . . said that?"

"That's right, he did. He told Bryan he has something to tell you, something important." She broke off abruptly. "Michelle, what's the matter? Did I say something wrong?"

"No. It isn't that." She felt sick suddenly. She felt as though she were about to faint.

"Is it so wrong that Rick is coming here?" Carla asked, puzzled. "You should be glad."

"It's Jim," she thought sickly. "He's heard. Jim's dead." She looked at Carla and as always when she needed words most, she could not find them.

"Michelle?"

"I'll listen to what Rick has to say, Carla," she said quietly.

"Good!" Carla said, relieved. "You do that, and everything will be just fine. You'll see."

"Yes," she said. "I'll make the coffee now. . ."

"Leave it. I'll fix it in a minute. You just sit down and talk to Bryan."

"No. I'll get it. I'm ready, and I'd sooner be doing something." Her attempted smile left Carla even more bewildered, but she escaped before Carla could take it any further.

Bryan looked up quickly as she came out. "Hello there, Michelle. Feeling better?"

"Yes, thanks."

"Good. Carla give you my message?"

"Yes, thanks." She busied herself in the kitchen, aware of Bryan's eyes following her, as puzzled as Carla's had been. "Was the meeting a success, Bryan?"

He frowned. "I wouldn't say it was. A lot of fuss for a few thousand dollars. There isn't a member on the board who hasn't given many times that. Still, it helps, so I suppose it's worthwhile. You know who the bene-factress was as well as I do, Michelle, and she'll spend more on trips in Europe this summer, you can bet on it."

"Miss Randolf is going to Europe?" she asked.

"That's right. But I have a feeling Rick wants to tell you about that. Michelle, Rick is very fond of you. He is also worried about you. I'm not quoting him on this, but that's the way it is, I assure you."

She set out the cups. "I . . . owe Rick a great deal. You've been very kind, and so has Carla."

"Neither kindness or thought of any debt comes into it with Rick, Michelle," he said gruffly. "Believe me, I *know* Rick. For both your sakes I hope that when he comes here today you can regain what you found here that first weekend. I believe you will, and so does Carla. We're keeping our fingers crossed for you both. Shall I take the tray out for you?"

The morning passed slowly. Michelle went through all the gestures of surfing, sunbaking, joining in their conversation. At another time she knew it would have been a gay and delightful morning. But today she could hardly keep her self-control. They delayed lunch, wait-ing for Rick. When he did not come Bryan bought sandwiches and milk at the store and they had a picnic on the beach.

When they became restless again and tried to persuade her to swim with them, Michelle shook her head. "You two go in. I'll go back to the cottage and have a sleep."

Michelle watched them run down the beach. Together they dived through the first breaker and she watched them swim out strongly, close together.

She walked back slowly to the cottage and went inside. She sat in one of the deep chairs staring toward Tern Isle.

Jim would have loved this place. He had always seemed like a kid let out of school on vacations in Florida. He was mad about the sea and anything connected with it.

Suddenly she heard a car stop on the road behind the house. She watched the door beyond the open kitchen. It had to be Rick, and he was a long time coming in. Perhaps he remembered what had been between them for a little while. That must make it difficult for him. Must make him hesitant out there. She began to feel sorry for him. He should know her better than that. There would be no tears. She would not embarrass him. She seldom gave way to tears where they could be seen. Her grief and her emotions always embarrassed her.

"Michelle?"

She started. He had walked around to the beach, to come up the front path. He was watching her from the doorway as she stood up quickly, almost as though he had been watching her while she stared so intently at the back door waiting for him.

"Hello, Rick!"

"Bryan gave you my message? Are they here?"

"No. You didn't see them at the beach?"

"I hoped you'd be here alone. Sit down, Michelle. I have something to tell you."

Here it is, she thought, and despite her resolutions she felt the panic grow in her. She sat down weakly.

"It's . . . about Jim, then?" she said quietly. "Rick, I've known that ever since Bryan said you were coming

102

here to see me today. You can tell me now. I . . . won't cry . . . or embarrass you."

He frowned at her angrily. "I don't understand you, Michelle. You're one of the most sensitive people I've ever known and yet. . ." He shook his head. "Yes, it's about your brother. He's alive, Michelle. He's had a bad time, and it isn't over yet, but he's alive."

She stared up at him in disbelief. "He's alive? Jim . . . is alive?" Her lips formed the words but he could not hear them.

"Yes," he said. "Your brother is alive. That's the first and most important thing for you to realize. He isn't a prisoner, although he has been one. He's safe in Hawaii, in the Naval hospital near Honolulu. Do you understand that?"

"Yes," Her lips formed the word. "I understand that. Thank God! Oh, thank God!"

"Michelle, are you all right? Michelle?" His voice seemed to be coming from a long way off.

She became aware slowly that he was holding a glass to her lips, and that he had spilt some of the contents and it was trickling down between her breasts. Her teeth chattered against the glass, and she pushed away the hand holding it.

"I'm all right!" she whispered. "I don't need that."

"Better put your head down for a while yet. You fainted."

"No!"

"Okay. Lean back then, and I'll get us *both* a drink. I think I need one almost as much as you do. You're not an easy girl to argue with, believe me. Even when you faint."

"I'd never argue with you, Rick. All I could ever feel for you is gratitude."

"*All!*" he said angrily. He pulled up a chair and sat facing her. "I received a report from Colonel Anderson last night, and afterwards I called him in Hawaii. I'd asked Mrs. Barton to watch out for the letter and she called me to say it was waiting in my office. Anderson had been working on it ever since he received my letter. He'd been using a number of channels that wouldn't interest you. One was concerned with men who through amnesia or other reasons, were unidentifiable. One case interested him. The man had been found when an airdrop of our guys overran a Vietcong base where they held some prisoners. It was quite a long way from where your brother was shot down, and the guy was in pretty bad shape and had no identification. There were three others with him, but none of them survived to reach our base. But they were Army men, so the conclusion reached by the men who found him was that this man was also from an Army unit."

"Was he . . . badly wounded?" she asked sickly.

"He'd been shot through the foot, and had a head wound that had apparently healed some time before. They flew him to Pleiku and Major Blight, a friend of mine, amputated the left foot because of gangrene."

"Gangrene?"

He avoided her eyes. "Yes. He'd walked a long way on that foot before the Vietcong caught him, and farther still as they moved their prisoners from place to place. He was down to eighty-three pounds, and that didn't help the soldier Anderson brought to Pleiku to identify him. But it was *thought* he was Lieutenant Lambert. The Navy moved in then but Anderson stayed with it. Two of the officers of your brother's squadron who knew him well had been returned to Hawaii, so they sent him there and Anderson went with him. Both men identified him as Lieutenant Lambert, although he couldn't recognize either of them."

"They're sure?"

"Yes, they're sure. The neurological people at Pearl Harbor believe that pressure from the head wound, a ridge of bone from the fracture that's grown together now, is pressing inward upon the brain and is the cause of the amnesia. If so, it can be relieved by trephine, as you must realize."

"When?" she whispered faintly.

"They intend to operate on Monday," he told her quietly.

104

"Tomorrow? So soon? Do you think he can stand it, Rick?" Her eyes appealed to him; she looked anxious and frightened.

"They know what they're doing. They've had him under observation. Would they risk it if he couldn't?"

"If the pressure was increasing, if there was increasing brain damage that could be . . terminal? Rick, you know better than I do what they'd do then?"

"If it was his only chance, no matter what his condition . . . yes, they'd operate. My reports have come from Colonel Anderson, not from the neurological surgeon. As far as I know, it is a simple trephine, and his condition warrants it. I can't tell you more than that, Michelle. I've been trying to contact your brother's surgeon. But it's Sunday in Hawaii too, so I can't get in touch. I'm expecting a call from him at my apartment tonight. I've arranged a few days' leave for you with Miss Pringle, and a seat is booked on tonight's plane for Hawaii. The plane leaves at two A.M. and arrives around seven. But they're not operating until afternoon, so you can see him before the operation, if you want to. Do you, Michelle?"

"Yes," she said. "Oh yes, Rick, please."

He nodded. "I thought you'd say that. Very well, I'll arrange everything. Have you told Carla about Jim?"

"No. I didn't want to inflict my troubles on her."

"No, you wouldn't."

The gentleness, the compassion in his eyes surprised her when she looked at him. "I'll have to explain to Carla now, though," she said.

He nodded. "Since you find it so difficult to confide in anyone, I'll walk down to the beach and tell them what's happening. You'll have time to pack while I'm away, and think over what I've told you. You'd prefer to be alone for that, wouldn't you?"

"Rick, I. . ."

"You don't have to explain anything Michelle," he said gently. "After I've brought the others back I'll drive you to the hospital to pack. But you will have to take a cab from the hospital to the airport. I'll have to

105

wait in my apartment for the call from Hawaii. I'll let you know what he says while you're at the airport. By phone if the call comes through too late, in person if there's time."

She said slowly: "I don't know how to thank you, Rick. You've been a wonderful, wonderful friend."

She watched the impulse to take her in his arms and kiss her form in his gray eyes, warming them subtly, holding her fascinated as she looked at him. She knew a surge of panic, and thought, No Rick! Don't! I couldn't bear it. Not just to lose you again.

She watched the impulse fade slowly. He went out without speaking again or looking back. She heard his footsteps receding as he walked down the path.

chapter nine

"Last call for passengers on flight twenty-one for Hawaii," the voice boomed over the amplifiers. "Flight twenty-one for Hawaii. Last call."

Michelle Lambert settled into her seat, glad that there was no one sitting beside her.

She closed her eyes and leaned back gratefully. Hawaii was a faraway place full of strange-sounding names. Islands she had never seen. She remembered a letter from Jim, written from Pearl Harbor and painting a vivid and glowing description of the island as seen through the eyes of a young and impressionable Navy flier.

To a girl spending most of her working life in an operating room it sounded like an earthly paradise. Jim had wanted her to spend that year's vacation in Hawaii, but it hadn't been possible. Soon after that he had been sent to a carrier and Vietnam.

Could that possibly have been only a year ago? So much had happened since that it seemed like a lifetime.

But she must not think of that. In five hours she would be in Hawaii. Jim was alive and she would see him there; five hours was not very long. She could keep her eyes closed and pretend to sleep.

"All clear," a voice called. Rubber tires rumbled. They were moving the steps away now.

The air hostess spoke somewhere close by. The seat next to her was no longer vacant; someone was sitting down, careful not to disturb her. She kept her eyes closed. Time enough to discover her companion when she had to fasten her seat belt. As the take-off instructions came over the amplifiers, she opened her eyes.

"Rick!"

He was watching her silently. He said quietly, "My call from Hawaii was late coming through. I wasn't sure that I'd make the flight."

"I . . . didn't know you intended to come with me. You didn't say that."

He smiled grimly. "Or ask you if it was okay with you. No Michelle, I did not. You would have tried to stop me if you'd known. You would have refused me if I'd asked. But did you really think I could allow you to go alone?"

"But your patients, Rick?" She was remembering with dismay the long surgery schedules.

"Hillside functioned without me for quite some time," he said. "It can do without me today, and maybe tomorrow and the next day. We'll see what happens in Hawaii. Let me help you with that."

Her fingers were fumbling with the catch of her seat belt. Momentarily he was very close to her as he bent across. Her eyes closed involuntarily. She heard the belt click, he straightened.

"Thanks. . ." she murmured.

"I knew you would have preferred someone else with you. Perhaps Carla, but there just wasn't time, and I have reasons of my own to go to Hawaii. I have a few loose ends to clear up with Colonel Anderson. I want to thank him in person for what he's done."

She leaned back for the take-off, closing her eyes. When the jet leveled out she found him still watching her. Now he would tell her what the surgeon had said. She waited apprehensively.

"Commander Gressor is operating, Michelle. I've never met him, but I know of him. He's a good man. The operation is scheduled for two thirty. He said that your brother's physical condition is surprisingly good, considering what he's been through."

"But the injury, Rick? Are there complications that make the operation necessary so soon?"

He hesitated. A hesitation that only she, knowing him so well, would have noticed.

"Gressor said there's some inflammation; either of the dura or of the brain itself beneath the ridge of bone that's creating the pressure. It's difficult to decide whether it's confined to the dura or extends to the brain itself. Gressor said it's a small area, but it is inflammation and it *is* spreading, and it seems to be meningeal. That makes it imperative that someone operate as soon as possible. On the evidence I have, I agree. It has to be done, Michelle. It's fortunate that your brother has come through his ordeal as well as he has. It is also fortunate that he has Commander Gressor for his surgeon. Better try to sleep now, Michelle. Everyone else is, and you'll need your strength today."

"I'll try. . ."

"I have some tablets here, if that would help?"

"No." He was the one who needed sleep, she decided, studying him. He looked exhausted. She reached out a hand and touched his. "Thank you for everything, Rick. Good night."

"Night," he said.

She closed her eyes at once, withdrawing her hand from his.

"Michelle?"

"Yes?" she asked.

"He's come so far. Have confidence now."

"Now that you've explained Jim's trouble to me and told me about Commander Gressor, I do have confidence."

It seemed a long time since he had seen her smile so warmly.

When his steady breathing deepened, Michelle opened her eyes and looked at him. Relaxed, he looked younger and somehow more vulnerable. It gave her a warm, protective feeling, watching him sleeping.

She sat there watching him contentedly for a long time, until the stars began to fade and the gray of dawn crept over the eastern sky.

Rick Prentice wakened startled. He was sweating and his heart pounded dully from dreaming. For a moment he thought himself in another jet at another time in another place, until he saw the civilian clothes of his fellow passengers and remembered Michelle.

He turned quickly and found her dark eyes watching him steadily.

"You've half an hour yet, Rick," she said, smiling at him.

He glanced at his watch automatically, then at the sun rising from the sea. He began to stretch his long legs.

"I must have needed that, Michelle," he said. He studied her more intently then, noticing the dark smudges under her eyes. He frowned. It had been a mistake allowing himself to fall asleep that way. He should have kept an eye on her, made sure she took a sleeping tablet.

He smiled at her ruefully. "Have you been awake long?"

"I didn't notice the time. But I had plenty of rest."

"I'll wash up and have the hostess bring us coffee. We're having breakfast with Anderson at his hotel. He's booked rooms for us there."

"Shall I see Jim then?"

"I'll call Gressor from the hotel and you can ask him. Don't be disappointed if that isn't possible, Michelle. Your brother will be having tests this morning, and being prepared for surgery. You'll see him before the operation, I promise you that; and again when it's over and he's out of the anesthesia."

"It's going to seem strange waiting it out, Rick; when I see him he'll be under sedation."

"Which might be better than seeing him awake, if he can't recognize you. Less strain on you. You won't be alone, waiting. I'll be with you. Now I'm going to get us some coffee."

Her seat was empty when he returned. She came back with her hair brushed and fresh makeup on as the hostess brought the coffee. Soon after that they watched the islands of Hawaii rise from the horizon; their smokey blues changing to the vivid green of vegetation, white sand and brown rock set in a blue sea.

Colonel Anderson, tall, lean and gray-haired was obviously pleased to meet Rick again as they shook hands.

"Your brother proved to be a hard man to find and identify, Miss Lambert. But as Rick has told you, there's no doubt at all about the identification. It is your brother we've found. Commander Gressor believes that the operation is going to make all the difference to him. He said he would prefer you not to see him until just before the operation. He'll be under sedation then, but as Gressor said, you will probably find that less upsetting than seeing him this morning."

The windows of her room looked down on the beach below. They both came in with her, while Rick called Commander Gressor.

Commander Gressor had a deep and pleasant voice. He said, "Dr. Prentice has told me that you are a nurse, Miss Lambert. If there's anything worrying you, anything you want to know, please feel free to ask me."

She said slowly: "I've been wondering about Jim's leg, Commander. Dr. Prentice said there was gangrene."

"Your brother was lucky, Miss Lambert. Apparently there was a clear line of demarcation, so they looked after that at Pleiku quite satisfactorily. You probably know as well as we do that sometimes surgeons are too conservative where gangrene is concerned. Major Bligh however has done an excellent job. He decided wisely that the foot must be amputated immediately. The amputation has healed well, and is giving no trouble. The operation was planned carefully for an artificial foot. I can't guarantee that he'll run a hundred yards in ten seconds, but there's no reason why he couldn't dance with a girl, play golf, swim, do most of the things

111

that young men of his age like to do—provided today's operation can give him the incentive to do these things."

She asked anxiously, "Is there a possibility that it may not?" She hesitated. "That his condition . . . increases the risk?"

"There's always an element of risk in any operation, Miss Lambert," Gressor said. "You know that. We'd prefer to wait until Lieutenant Lambert is physically stronger, but unfortunately that isn't possible. The meningeal infection is spreading. We're holding it, but we don't know for how long. It had reached a critical stage when he was brought here. It's my considered opinion, and that of my colleagues, that delay now is a far greater risk than immediate operation. Your brother's strength and resistance are low. We've done everything possible to build him up, but we've run out of time. However, there is another side to it, and one you should think about. There are people who have an inner strength, a toughness, a resistance to disease, wounds and pain, that other people don't have. Your brother survived alone and badly wounded in the jungle for what we believe now to be many weeks. He survived capture by the Vietcong. Considering these things it is my personal belief that he will survive the operation. That's all I wanted to say, unless you have any more questions?"

"No, Commander. You've been patient with me, and very kind. I have every confidence in you."

"Thank you, Miss Lambert. I'll see you as quickly as I can afterward. Do you have someone to wait with you?"

"Yes, I have."

"If you feel up to it, I'd like you to be in the recovery room with me when he comes out."

"I will."

"Good girl!" he said, heartily. "Better rest as much as you can this morning. Good-bye."

She put the phone down. Her eyes met Rick's and he smiled at her reassuringly. "Gressor impress you favorably?"

112

"I feel a lot better about it now, Rick."

"Good. Now you're going to take these tablets, and you're going to sleep until noon."

"You won't let me oversleep?"

"No. I promise." His eyes made her think that there was a lot more he was about to say, but he turned abruptly and went out with Colonel Anderson.

She had barely noticed the room before but she saw now as she looked around that it was very comfortable. Two chairs faced the open windows side by side. She sank into the nearest. Catamarans with brightly colored sails were moving smoothly just beyond the breakers, their decks crowded with people in gay swim suits.

She had expected to see huge breakers roaring in, but the sea was calm, the breakers no larger than they'd been at Silver Sands. She watched a couple going into the water hand in hand. "If this was over," she thought, "how wonderful it would be to walk into the surf like that with Rick. . ."

Only that was impossible now, of course. The thread between them was broken. She would be a fool to think otherwise, or judge his kindness to be love. Her eyes filled with tears, and the people and the blue sea blurred and were gone. . .

She cried for what seemed a long time, and then she was dreaming. The dream was so pleasant that she decided she did not want to wake. It seemed that Rick was carrying her in his arms, holding her gently, and the things he was muttering angrily were laced with terms of endearment that made her want to cry again. She supposed he was carrying her along the beach at Silver Sands, or from the water as he had carried her the night she almost drowned.

When he put her down she sank so deeply into the sand that it was like the softest bed ever. He began taking off her shoes and covering her gently with what felt like a silk sheet.

He stood looking down at her then a long time. She could not see him, but she knew he was there. She knew that he was going to kiss her when he bent very slowly

113

and for a brief moment she felt the pressure of his lips lightly on hers. . .

She wakened reluctantly. Her head felt as if it were full of cotton. The dryness in her mouth she knew came from the sedation. Someone was pulling up shades that allowed bright light to stream into the room, and she could smell the fragrance of coffee.

The girl who turned toward her from the windows was smiling cheerfully.

"You awake now, Miss Lambert? Dr. Prentice gave me the key and said I was to call you and that you were to drink this coffee. He said you don't need to hurry. There is plenty of time; he will be in the lounge when you come down."

She thanked the girl, and sat up groggily, grateful for the strong black coffee. There was plenty of it and she began to feel better with the second cup.

She discovered that she was lying on the large bed in the hotel room, fully dressed except for her shoes. She decided that the sedation must have been strong, very strong, for she had no memory of falling asleep here. The last she remembered was sitting on a chair staring down at the beach.

She put the empty cup down and swung her legs off the bed. At least the coffee had revived her and she felt better for her sleep. She was thinking more clearly now. Heavens, what time was it?

She remembered that her small leather-covered traveling clock was still in her bag. She opened the bag quickly. Five minutes past twelve. Rick had kept his word. Time to change her crumpled clothes, to shower and freshen up.

Rick was sipping a drink alone in a corner of the lounge as she came from the elevator. He was frowning at the drink as though he disliked it and drinking it was making him feel miserable.

She began to walk toward him and as though he felt her presence he looked up quickly and smiled.

"That's better!" he said in a pleased voice. "Sleep makes a difference. They say too that dressing up is good for a girl's morale. Right now you're a different girl from the one I gave sedation to four hours ago. You look terrific in that dress. I have a car waiting outside. Like a drink before we leave? One might help."

He thought of everything. She smiled at him gratefully. "I'll be okay now, Rick, thank you. But finish your drink."

He shook his head. "I didn't really want it. All it was doing was make me feel sorry for myself."

"I don't see why? I mean, there's no reason for you to feel that way, is there Rick?" she asked him smiling.

"I have plenty to regret. But let's just go. There could be delays at the hospital. . ."

What he had said sobered Michelle abruptly. She had forgotten Bernice for a little while, but Rick had not. Rick was regretting being here, so far from Bernice. The kindness that had brought him here with her was something he was beginning to regret.

She sat beside him, subdued, as he drove across town toward the hospital. He was quiet for a while, then as he noticed her silence he began to talk about the passing scene. She answered mechanically, pretending interest, knowing that all he was doing was trying to distract her attention from the hospital ahead, and her coming ordeal.

She felt better at the hospital. The modern building was reassuring. The nurses were like nurses anywhere except for the different uniform. Rick asked the questions, with people answering him respectfully. She followed where he led. They were on the surgical floor then and he was talking to a senior nurse.

"Lieutenant Lambert? Yes, of course. It's Colonel Prentice and Miss Lambert, isn't it? Commander Gressor said I was to expect you. He asked me to tell you that he'll see you before he goes up to the O.R."

"Miss Lambert would like to see her brother, Lieutenant Madison," Rick said, smiling at the nurse. "And it isn't Colonel any more. It's just Doctor."

"Yes, Doctor. Are you coming in with Miss Lambert?"

Rick glanced at her. "I think Miss Lambert might prefer to see her brother alone. Do you know where Commander Gressor is? I'd like to talk to him while Miss Lambert is with her brother."

She listened numbly to their conversation. The nurse began talking to her again then, guiding her down a passage.

"This is the waiting room, Miss Lambert. Commander Gressor will see you in there before he goes to the operating room. I understand you're a nurse, so you'll realize that your brother is already under sedation. You have twenty minutes before he goes upstairs. I'll leave you with him and come back to take you to the waiting room. This way please. . ."

She stood very still staring at the man in the bed as the nurse closed the door behind her. It was not her brother lying there so still, it was a wasted caricature of her brother, a creature of skin and bone with a shaven head bearing a livid scar. The arms that lay upon the sheet had swollen wrists and claws for fingers. The skin on his face was thickened, and had a bluish tinge over the bony prominences.

"Oh Jim, Jim. . . !" she sobbed.

Commander Gressor had lied to her about his belief in some hidden source of strength. No man who looked as her brother did could survive an operation. The signs of malnutrition, of deadly weakness were only too apparent. Rick would know that if he saw him.

Jim was going to die. . .

It seemed only moments before the nurse came back, and she was being helped toward the waiting room.

"Are you all right, Miss Lambert? Shall I bring you a stimulant? I'll contact Dr. Prentice and get him down here at once."

"I'm quite all right, thank you," she heard herself say. "Please don't worry Dr. Prentice, Lieutenant."

She understood the nurse's haste in leaving her. The relatives of people about to be operated on were always more trying than the patient. You were glad to walk

116

away from them. She had felt that way herself many times.

Only it was different when it was you; it was vastly different. Rick was with Commander Gressor when he came into the waiting room. Gressor was a burly man with a lined, strong face and prematurely gray hair. He said a lot of reassuring things to Michelle that she listened to and agreed with mechanically in order to be polite. It didn't matter what he said; now she *knew*, she knew just how bad it was.

Commander Gressor was going. Rick walked out into the passage and she could hear the murmur of their voices before Rick came back.

She became aware that Rick had taken hold of her hands and was holding them still.

"This is where we sweat it out," he said quietly. "It isn't going to be easy for you, no matter what I say. But it will be less difficult if you relax. I told you on the phone last night that I'd changed my opinion about your brother's chances. Where's that faith of yours I spoke of then? I haven't changed my mind about that, Michelle. After talking to Gressor and reading your brother's case history I still believe that Gressor is going to bring him through."

"You haven't seen Jim, Rick. . ."

"No. But I've seen his chart and I've seen other men suffering from malnutrition and wounds. I've seen a great many of them, Michelle. I've seen men in worse physical shape than your brother; men that secretly I gave no chance at all. And I've watched some of them make what seemed to me a miraculous recovery. It was not my skill that brought them through, it was some sort of hidden strength within themselves that just wouldn't let them give up."

"But Jim doesn't know, he doesn't reason any more. . ."

"Maybe. But if he has that hidden reserve of strength, he does not have to direct it, it's built-in. We're not going to talk about that any more. It's out of our hands

117

now. Tell me about your brother. Didn't you mention surfing with him in Florida once. . ."

She began to talk about Jim, and there was relief in telling him, as he had hoped there might be.

She became calm, and he released her hands. They were waiting together now, like friends. It was a longer wait than she had expected. If he had been operating instead of Gressor it would be over now, she decided when the second hour had passed. She wished he had been able to; that she might have been able to take her brother away from here, to Hillside.

He had taken hold of one of her hands and was holding it firmly. He said quietly, "Here is Commander Gressor now, Michelle."

He steadied her as she stood up quickly. Gressor still wore gown and cap, and his mask hung down beneath his chin so that Michelle knew he had come to them as soon as it ended; waiting only to pull off his gloves. He looked exhausted, but he was smiling.

"He's through it, Miss Lambert," he said quietly. "His pressure is reasonably good, and so are pulse and respiration. They're taking him through to the recovery room now, and I'm going back there to stay with him for a while. At this stage I'd say the operation was successful."

"Thank God," she whispered. She felt Rick's hands steadying her, Gressor was looking at her sympathetically.

He said gruffly, "As for his mental condition, when he comes out of the anesthesia, we'll know about that. Do you have the strength to be there, to help us?"

Rick answered for her. "She has both the strength and the courage, Commander."

Gressor glanced at him, and nodded. "You know where the recovery room is. I'd like you to be there, Prentice. I would have liked to have you in the operating room with me. Lieutenant Madison will fix you both up with masks, gowns and caps. You'll have to excuse me now. I'll expect you in the recovery room within the next half hour."

118

He went out briskly and Michelle sank back on the hard waiting room seat.

Rick said exultantly, "I told you Gressor was a good man! Michelle, are you all right?"

"I will be in a moment, Rick. It was just the relief I guess." She shook her head. "It's been a long day, and it isn't over yet."

"So now we both know what it's like to be on the other side of the counter," he said. "Let's go. The recovery room is on the next floor."

There was something reassuring in the familiar routine of donning gown, cap and mask with Rick. It made her feel like a nurse again. In a way it made her anxiety seem a less personal thing.

Lieutenant Madison came into the room. "I heard your brother came through the operation quite well, Miss Lambert," she said cheerfully. "Feel better now?"

"Yes, thank you."

"Good. The Commander is in the recovery room. Your brother was still out when I looked in just now, but he's starting to move, so it shouldn't be long. This way please. . ."

It was all familiar: the oxygen, the transfusion feeding into a vein of the leg, the bandaged head moving restlessly, even the patient's skeletal face; for she had seen cancer patients in as weakened a condition when their disease was terminal. The difference was that this patient was Jim.

"I think we'll have a little more oxygen now, Sam," Commander Gressor was saying as Lieutenant Madison opened the door.

"Miss Lambert and Dr. Prentice are here, Commander."

"Good," he said without looking round. "Come in. Won't be a minute. Our boy is just starting to become restless, Sam. I think that should do, don't you?"

"Yes, Commander," the anesthetist took away the oxygen.

"Later we might use an oxygen tent, but not right now," Gressor said. "Pressure? Yes, that's fair enough.

119

Pulse? No change. Don't go away, Sam. Even though it looks as though everything is under control." He straightened and turned to look at Michelle. "Well, here he is, and as you see, we haven't given him too bad a time back there. He's due to start taking interest in people and things around him very soon now."

Jim began to move his head from side to side slowly. His eyelids fluttered, closed again, and he began muttering incomprehensible words.

"Come over here, Prentice," Gressor said. "Do you understand what he's saying?"

Rick moved closer, bending beside Gressor.

Rick said slowly, "Yes! Yes I do. He's speaking Vietnamese. He's begging for food. Now . . . his foot. He says his foot hurts. He says he can't stand the pain." Rick's voice faded as he remembered Michelle. "He thinks he's still in the jungle, a prisoner."

Please, Michelle prayed silently. Please God let him know me! Let his mind heal with his body. . .

"Mayday, Mayday" a voice mumbled. "The stick's dead and every warning light on the goddam panel red. . ."

"Lieutenant Lambert, can you hear me? *Lambert!* You're okay now. You're safe. Lambert, wake up!"

Michelle waited tensely, unable to see her brother's face from where she sat. She could see the foot of the bed though. Jim was lying on his back, and she could see the way one foot tented the sheet. On the other side the sheet lay flat.

"Lieutenant Lambert! Can you hear me? You're safe. Can you understand what I'm saying? You're safe! You're among friends."

"Who . . . are you?" It was a weak voice, so low that Michelle could hardly hear it.

"My name is Gressor, Lambert." Gressor bent closer to his patient. "Commander Gressor. I'm a doctor and we've been looking after you. Do you know where you are? You're in hospital in Hawaii. Can you understand that?"

120

"At . . . Pearl Harbor?" The weak voice sounded surprised.

"That's right, Lambert. At Pearl Harbor. You've been ill, and you've had surgery, but everything is going to be fine now. Can you understand that? You're safe. You're in hospital in Hawaii, and you're going to get well."

"I . . . understand, sir," Jim answered hesitantly.

"Good boy! I've someone who wants to see you now. She's a nurse, and you know her well. I want you to tell me who she is. She's worried about you and she's come a long way to see you. Here she is now. . ."

Rick had hold of her arm and was leading her toward the bed. She needed the support of his arm, but when she reached the bed she stood alone, standing very straight and looking down calmly at the man on the bed.

"Hello, Jim," she said.

He stared up at her vaguely, his eyes uncertain, the pupils dilated.

"Nurse. . . ?" he whispered.

Gressor said, "I think under the circumstances we'll dispense with the mask for a moment, shall we?"

She loosened the mask and brought it down beneath her chin, holding her breath as she looked down at him. He seemed to be straining forward, trying to see her better. He was having difficulty in focusing his eyes upon her face.

"Michelle?" he muttered. "Michelle, is it really you. . . ?"

Gressor said in an authoritative voice, "Lieutenant, you know who this is?"

His eyes did not move from her face. "My . . . sister, sir," he whispered. "It's . . . been a long time."

"And a hard time, Lieutenant. But everything is going to be just fine now. That's all you have to think about. We're going to take you back to your own room soon, and your sister will stay with you there for a little while. But you must rest and conserve your strength. So not too much reminiscing, eh?"

Lieutenant Lambert said weakly: "No, sir." But his eyes never left Michelle's face.

The bond between them was a very strong one, Rick Prentice decided. This man adored his sister. He looked away, embarrassed. Michelle had slipped the mask back. Her brown eyes were full of tears.

Gressor said in a low voice, "We've a few things to do here yet, Miss Lambert. Give us another hour and then you can see your brother in his room for a few minutes."

Her eyes told her brother that she was smiling at him. "I'll see you again soon, Jim," she said cheerfully. "You must rest and get well quickly. Everything is going to be fine."

He tried to return her smile. "Whatever you say, Sis. Whatever you . . . say . . ."

His eyes closed wearily then, and Rick led her outside. "Commander Gressor is quite a guy," he said.

"He was wonderful."

They went down in the elevator and along the passage to the familiar waiting room. She walked inside and he closed the door behind her.

"An hour?" she said uneasily.

He nodded. "There are several things we can do. Anderson will be anxious to know what has happened, and he deserves to know. I can call him from in here. I can also call the restaurant downstairs and have them bring up some coffee. I guess we can both use some. Okay?"

"Yes, Rick."

"Your brother will be drowsy when you see him again. They'll have given him sedation to keep him resting and immobilized. But at least you'll have the satisfaction of being with him, and of knowing that your faith was justified."

"It will be good just to see him."

"Good for him too. There will be a lot of other times, Michelle. Each time he will be a little better, a little stronger, a little more like the brother you knew."

"I'm sure of that now." She looked at him. "But I

wasn't before, Rick. At Silver Sands you believed he'd never be found. I had the same thought when I saw it in your eyes, and again this morning when I saw Jim. I was sure then that he . . . would die. A woman doesn't always express the things she feels in words, Rick," she said quietly. "Or mean everything she says."

"I see," he said. "Well, that encourages me to say something I've been wanting to say ever since you started dropping my instruments in the operating room. I'm going to say it *now*, before I call Anderson or send for coffee. It's about Bernice Randolf and the clinic."

"Rick, you don't have to explain, not to me. You've been more than kind, and if you want to fly back tonight to San Francisco, I'll understand. You've done far too much for Jim and me already."

"You're not going to get rid of me *that* easily, Michelle," he said grimly. "I'm going back when you do, not before!"

"But Bernice. . . ? Rick I don't *want* you to go. And I didn't mean to offend you by suggesting it. But if you and Bernice. . ."

"Bernice left for Europe this morning," he said. "And I understand she isn't coming back for quite some time. That's okay with me. It's what she needs. She's had a serious operation. Now will you answer a question for me please?"

"I'll try, Rick," she murmured.

"Okay. Could you have kissed me the way you did on the boat at Silver Sands if you hadn't . . . been in love with me?"

He had asked it angrily, but the warmth, the tenderness in his eyes was more difficult to face than anger. She looked away, uncertainly.

"Michelle?" he demanded harshly.

"No Rick, I couldn't . . ." she whispered.

"So what made you change?" he demanded. "Those stupid rumors about Bernice and me? Or do you usually blow hot and cold that way, loving a guy one day, detesting him the next?"

"Rick, you're being cruel. I haven't changed. It was

you. Oh, I don't blame you! Bernice is . . . very attractive."

"She's not as attractive to me as you are," he said deliberately. He put his hands on her shoulders and turned her so that she had to face him. "You've been around hospitals a long time, Michelle. You must have seen women patients who became infatuated with their doctors before, surely?"

"Yes, of course, but Bernice. . ."

"Without the doctors falling in love with them?"

"Yes. . ." she faltered.

"Then I was right," he said. "I've been doubting it lately, but I was right. I wasn't just making a fool of myself."

"I . . . don't understand."

"Bernice was upset of course," he said. "She's a rather conceited girl. She's spoiled and always had her own way, but she'll get over it. The gift she gave us for the clinic, even if it might have been larger, is still sufficient to help us considerably. Later, with Arthur Dickinson's maternity wing functioning, the clinic can stand on its own feet."

She said uncertainly, "Rick, what *are* you saying?"

"That I wasn't just being a conceited fool when I told Bernice I was in love with another girl and intended to marry her, since I believed that the girl felt the same way about me."

"Rick!" she gasped. "Are you saying. . ."

"Yes, it's you I'm talking about," he said. "My darling, sensitive, foolish little Michelle. I love you, and I want to marry you. I've felt that way about you ever since I kissed you on Dad's old fishing boat at Silver Sands. And since you've admitted you feel the same way, that's what we're going to do just as soon as your brother is out of danger and able to attend the wedding. Then we're going to spend our honeymoon here in Hawaii."

Instantly she was in his arms and he was kissing her. But when she could, she said quite firmly, "No, Rick!"

He held her away from him, staring at her face in dismay. "What was that? You don't mean . . ."

"Not in Hawaii, Rick," she said softly. "There's only one place for us. Silver Sands."

"Of course, darling Michelle," he said. "Of course. That will make it perfect." His lips touched hers, speaking more eloquently than they ever had with words.

Other SIGNET Nurse-Doctor Romances You Will Enjoy